DATE DUE

C.99	an	rh	ar
0.99	wf		
R.00			

SOMEONE
SPECIAL

SOMEONE SPECIAL

•

Gail MacMillan

AVALON BOOKS
THOMAS BOUREGY AND COMPANY, INC.
401 LAFAYETTE STREET
NEW YORK, NEW YORK 10003

© Copyright 1998 by Gail MacMillan
Library of Congress Catalog Card Number: 98-96333
ISBN 0-8034-9313-4

PRINTED IN THE UNITED STATES OF AMERICA
ON ACID-FREE PAPER
BY HADDON CRAFTSMEN, BLOOMSBURG, PENNSYLVANIA

To Charlene . . . who knows how to be a friend.

Chapter One

"Special!? Don't call me special! You don't know what special means!" Jason jumped to his feet and glared down at Ceilidh, fury electrifying every inch of his freckled face.

"Jason, please sit down." The young woman's soft brown eyes were imploring. "Let me explain."

"Yeah, right!" The thirteen-year-old, the peak of his baseball cap slanting down the back of his neck, baggy T-shirt and sweatpants half covered with a man's faded plaid shirt, was in no mood to listen. "If you're so great at picking out someone spe-

1

cial, why aren't you married or engaged or something?''

Furious, he turned away and marched defiantly on dirty high-tops toward the door.

''Jason, please wait!'' Ceilidh arose and reached after him but the door slammed on her words.

For a moment she stared at the closed panel; then, with a sigh so deep that it seemed to come from the tips of her toes, she sank back into her chair.

Whatever made me think I could handle this project? she thought defeatedly. She gazed around the neat, modern schoolroom and felt overwhelmed. What will I tell Mrs. Blackwell? she asked herself, remembering the day she had been hired to conduct this educational experiment.

''You're exactly the kind of teacher I want for this position, Ceilidh,'' Karen Blackwell, the regional director of education, had said as she sat perched on the edge of her polished mahogany desk and looked squarely at the eager, bright-eyed young teacher in front of her. ''You're clever, you love children, and you're not afraid of a challenge. I've stuck my neck out further than I care to think by devising and promoting this project. I can't risk its success on just anyone. That's why I've chosen you.''

''I'll do my best, Mrs. Blackwell,'' Ceilidh had said, her face reflecting avid interest in the mysterious project.

She knew how fortunate she had been to land a teaching job, any teaching job, her first year out of university, but now Karen Blackwell was telling her that not only was she hired, she was about to be given an extremely important position.

''Good. Let me explain.'' Tall, dark, slender, and attractive, the director exuded grace, sophistication, and confidence as she slid smoothly off her desk and went to sit in the big leather armchair behind it.

''As you may be aware, there has been a move afoot recently in the Department of Education toward school consolidation,'' she said, steepling her fingertips in front of her. ''In many cases that means closing small, rural schools and busing children long distances to town or city facilities. I don't believe a travel time of over an hour to class is acceptable for young students. It exhausts many children. Moreover, it throws them into a totally foreign environment far too early in their academic careers.

"I firmly believe young students do their best work in their home community. Toward this end I've fought long and hard to keep all rural schools in my jurisdiction open and have even gone a step further. I've advocated building a small, state-of-the-art version of the old one-room, one-teacher, kindergarten-to-grade-nine-school as an experimental proving ground in one of the rural areas under my supervision."

She paused and smiled at the slender, chestnut-haired young woman whose attractive oval face and wide brown eyes were bright with anticipation.

"Last autumn, much to my delight, the Department of Education decided to put my theory to the test. They agreed to construct such a building at Bay River, a tiny community about an hour's drive from here. This facility will provide data on which to base future rural school closures and, as a result, could prompt a whole new way of thinking about small country schoolhouses. If the students do better than their bused counterparts, my theory will be vindicated and at least a few rural schools may be saved. It will be your job to prove—or disprove—my theory. You, Ceilidh Highland, will be their teacher.''

Ceilidh swallowed a gasp. She hadn't been anticipating an assignment of this magnitude her first time out.

''Just a bit of background on Bay River itself,'' Karen Blackwell, apparently oblivious to the young teacher's state of shock, continued. ''The community recently appeared in the media because a couple of resident fishermen were suspected of using their boats to help smugglers import illegal drugs. That, however, should be of no concern to you. I very much doubt that the parents of any of your students are involved in this illicit business.''

''I'm grateful for your confidence, Mrs. Blackwell,'' Ceilidh finally managed to say, hoping she sounded cool and confident. She had barely heard the director's account of Bay River's drug trafficking problems she had been in such a state of astonishment at the magnitude of her posting. ''I'll do my best. I'll begin by driving down there this afternoon and finding living accommodations. I'd like to get settled in as soon as possible.''

''That won't be necessary,'' her employer replied. ''The province has even gone so far as to provide a renovated farmhouse for the teacher courageous enough to take on this job. It's a lovely old turn-of-the-century place that has lost none of its charm in the restoration process. It's not isolated, either. A road that leads to the wharf where the local fishermen tie up their boats runs at right angles from Coastal Highway 103 to the beach past the farm. You'll be able to watch all the comings and goings both on the main road and on the one to the shore. You'll love it. There's only one small catch.''

''Small catch?'' Ceilidh was apprehensive. The house had sounded too good to be true.

''It's a big house with three bedrooms upstairs.'' Karen Blackwell spoke slowly, watching the young teacher's reaction. ''Since the province is paying the rent, I had to agree that other government employees can stay in the extra rooms if the need arises . . . which it probably won't. Do you see that as a major problem?''

"No." Ceilidh was determined to keep her unruffled demeanor. "I've lived in a college dorm for the past four years. I'm accustomed to less than complete privacy in my living situation."

"Good. You can move in anytime. Probably the sooner the better since school starts next week. And Ceilidh?" Karen Blackwell arose and looked intently over at her.

"Yes?"

"You're not going to be lonesome down there, are you? I mean, you're not leaving any significant other, anyone special behind? I wouldn't want my chosen protégée to be kept from total concentration on the task because she's discontent."

"There's definitely no problem that way," Ceilidh said a bit more vehemently that she had intended and immediately hoped the director hadn't noticed.

"Fine," the older woman replied and came around her desk to offer Ceilidh her hand. "Good luck. I'll be looking forward to your reports."

Ceilidh could still see the confidence mirrored in Karen Blackwell's expression.

The director believed in her, trusted her; now she was letting her down after only one week on the job. This wonderful experiment in teaching was going to hit a brick wall and it would be all Ceilidh Highland's fault.

With a heavily aching heart, Ceilidh wandered slowly out of the schoolroom and paused in the hallway to look sadly about. A short seven days ago she had viewed this remarkable little school with pride and anticipation. Now it was darkened both by a storm blowing in off the bay and the agony of defeat smoldering in her chest.

It was a wonderful school, nevertheless, she knew. To her right was the door to a well-equipped gymnasium. To her left was the kitchen–dining room area complete with electric range, refrigerator, and microwave oven. Its rock maple tables and chairs were suggestive of a cozy country kitchen.

Farther along the corridor was the state-of-the-art computer lab with connections to the Internet and e-mail that also housed a wide-screen television set with VCR linked to a satellite dish on the roof. At the rear of this high-tech room was her office resplendent with wide oak desk, easy chairs for guests, filing cabinets, bookcases, and private washroom.

Ceilidh was appreciative of each of these rooms but the library just inside the school's main entrance was her favorite. This part of the school had been designed to exude a family room ambience. Brightened by several large bay windows, it contained couches, tables, and even padded window seats with views of the meadow and bay beyond. Books appropriate to all the age levels she taught filled the many shelves along the walls. There was even excellent stereo equipment housed in an entertainment center at the back of the room.

When she had first seen the library she had been elated. She had pictured herself seated in one of the window seats on a winter's afternoon, her eager-eyed, attentive students sitting on the floor about her as she read to them while classical music played softly in the background.

Now she sighed as she looked out into the big, empty room. Who had she thought she was going to be, she wondered ruefully, Snow White surrounded by thirteen enthralled little people? *Face the facts,* she told herself harshly. *This is the real world, not a fairy tale. There are no attentive children to cluster around you and definitely no Prince Charming ready to help you out of your troubles.*

Slowly she made her way to her office and sank into the suddenly too-big chair behind the desk. *I'm a failure,* she thought dejectedly. *I can't even handle a disruptive thirteen-year-old. Karen Blackwell thought I was someone special but she was wrong.* She pulled a Kleenex from a box on top of a small pile of correspondence and blew her nose.

Ceilidh Highland, stop feeling sorry for yourself this instant! a little voice inside rebuked her. *You've got more spunk than this!*

Do I? she asked silently. *I'm not sure anymore.*

Then, with an effort that seemed to sap the last of her flagging emotional strength, she forced herself back to the duties at hand. Knowing she had to check her e-mail before leaving for the weekend, she went into the computer lab. There might be communication from the district education office in town that required her immediate attention. She sat down before the monitor and snapped on the computer.

There was nothing from the home office, but there was a message from her parents. Retired and living in southern New Brunswick, the couple were blissfully happy with their new lifestyle and immensely proud of Ceilidh's accomplishments as both an honors university graduate and a teacher entrusted with a key position in her district.

Their message reflected this happiness so completely Ceilidh could not bring herself to tell them her actual state of being. They had earned a satisfying and contented retirement; she would not ruin it with her tale of agony and defeat.

She put her fingers to the keyboard and sent off a bright, cheerful little note, concluding with "Will write again on Monday. Love you both. Ceilidh."

Then in her mind she returned to her first week of school and her pupils, all thirteen of them. She saw Trevor, her single kindergartner, overactive, seemingly oblivious to her and even her slightest request. Attention deficit disorder, she decided tiredly. Then there was eight-year-old Ben struggling valiantly but hopelessly against some type of learning disability Ceilidh had yet to pinpoint.

And finally there was Jason, her nemesis, belligerent, sneering, bitterly unhappy, and out to make the rest of the world pay. Goodness, what was she to do? She couldn't resign. Not if she ever planned to hold any teaching position ever again; she had a contract to fulfill.

Wearily she packed her books, picked up her tan blazer, and turned off the lights. After activating the security system, she locked the door and walked away from her beloved little school.

Pausing for a moment in the parking lot, she clutched her schoolbooks tightly in her arms and turned her flushed, unhappy face toward the bay, gray and white-capped, a hundred yards beyond the school. Roiling charcoal clouds tumbled about overhead, threatening rain as they glowered down on a rising wind that bent the grass in the deserted pastureland to the right and sent anxious whispers rising through the tall pines to her left.

Standing alone beside her small black car, Ceilidh wished she had someone to talk to, to confide in, to discuss her disheartening dilemma with; someone caring and concerned; someone . . . special.

But she didn't. There was only a big, empty farmhouse to go back to with no one waiting to listen to her, to share with her, to console her.

It was her own fault, she told herself as she slid into her car and started the engine. During her college days, she had had numerous opportunities to add a significant other to her life. Ceilidh Highland, with her vibrant good looks and vivacious personality, had attracted more than her share of young men willing to play that role in her life. None, however, had proven to be exactly what she was looking for.

Maybe Jason is right, she thought dejectedly as she paused to look both ways before she pulled out onto the highway. *Maybe I won't recognize my someone special when he does come along. Maybe I've already missed him, maybe . . .*

With a deep sigh she put all speculation aside for the moment and drove out onto the highway. Right now she had bigger concerns than finding her Prince Charming.

Chapter Two

Stretched out in a full run, the big black horse burst around the corner of the barn directly into the path of the oncoming car. His rider, in an effort to avoid a collision, spun the animal sharply about in the same instant Ceilidh smashed her foot down on the brake. The horse's cries of alarm and the dull skid of dragging rubber filled the air. Tires and hooves threw up a huge cloud of dust and, for a moment, Ceilidh couldn't see what had become of the pair she had almost run into. Horrified, she leaped out of the car and tried to get a look at them as the dirt settled.

"What do you think you're doing? Are you crazy? And who are you anyway? What are you doing here? Don't you know this is private property? This is my house, I live here!" Relieved when she saw the rider dismounting unharmed, she became enraged and launched into a tirade of questions.

"Are you okay?" Ignoring her anger, the man quieted the prancing horse and turned to face her. And Ceilidh received a major surprise.

He had to be one of the handsomest men she had ever seen, movie stars not excepted. Tall, broad shouldered, and narrow waisted, the man who stood before her could have given any of the current romantic screen actors hard competition in the looks category. Dusty and windblown from his wild ride, he had all the appeal of a hero in any of the Western films Ceilidh had ever seen. He shoved dark, wavy hair back from his forehead and looked at her, deep concern mirrored in his brown eyes.

"Yes, yes, yes!" The tension of her first week at a new job and now this near accident had torn Ceilidh's nerves to shreds. This guy might be an Adonis but he was also an idiot who had very nearly caused a terrible accident, and she wasn't about to forgive him. "Can't you . . . can't you see I'm just fine?"

Then, suddenly, to her chagrin, she was crying, sobbing, humiliated by her lack of self-control but unable to stop.

"Hey!" He dropped the reins, leaving the horse ground tied, and in a few quick strides was at her side, his hand on her quaking shoulders. "It's okay. We're okay. That's all that matters."

"R-right!" She was sarcastic as she lurched free and fumbled in her skirt pocket for a Kleenex. "Everything is just hunky-dory."

"Come on," he said gently. "Help me turn Special out into the paddock. You look as if you could do with some fresh air."

"Turn Special . . . him?"—she gestured toward the horse—"out into the paddock . . . my paddock?" Ceilidh managed to come up to speed on their conversation. She blew her nose. "Why should you be turning him out into my paddock?"

"The province rents this place, doesn't it?" he asked, looking at her with intense brown eyes, and Ceilidh felt the impact of his gaze as distinctly as if he had touched her. Get a grip, she told herself.

"Yes," she said apprehensively. "But . . ."

"With the condition that other government employees can share the facilities from time to time if space allows?"

"Yes," she repeated. "But . . ."

"Well, I'm a government employee and I've just gotten permission to keep Special in the barn."

"Just exactly what sort of government employee are you, Mr. . . . ? Ceilidh struggled to get back to normality.

"Allan Dumont," he introduced himself. "Constable Allan Dumont. My friends call me Al. I'm with the local RCMP. Corporal Harry Aimes and I make up the constabulary in this area."

"A policeman." Ceilidh breathed tiredly, totally exasperated. No other fact could have destroyed any appeal the man might have had for Ceilidh as utterly and completely. She had loved a police officer once; she never would again, she had vowed one stormy January night five years ago.

"Come on, Miss Highland . . . that's

your name, isn't it? They told me a Miss Ceilidh Highland was the sole occupant of this farm.'' Oblivious to her inner revulsion, he gathered up the horse's reins and jerked his head in the direction of the barn. ''Keep me company while I put Special away. It'll help you unwind.''

He started to lead the horse away. Ceilidh began to follow automatically, then stopped abruptly.

''What makes you think I need to unwind?'' she asked crossly, hands on her slim hips. ''I'm fine, just fine.''

He paused and glanced back over his shoulder, a tormenting grin on that movie-star face.

''Well, if you're that scared of horses, then maybe you'd better stay where you are.''

''Scared of horses!'' As he started off again, Ceilidh was in full angry pursuit. ''What makes you think I'm scared of horses? Listen, Nelson Eddy, I'll have you know I'm a better-than-average rider myself. My dad taught me. He was an Olympic-class equestrian. Afraid of horses! As if!''

Indignantly Ceilidh followed Constable

Allan Dumont around to the stable door where a gray Jeep, which she previously hadn't been able to see, was parked and followed him and his horse into the barn. There she managed to wait patiently as he removed the animal's bridle, slipped a halter over its ears, and tied it in crossties in the stable's walkway.

Although she hated to admit it, she felt her anger and dejection clearing as she watched. She loved animals, especially horses. Just being around them had a reassuring, calming effect on her. Slowly she walked up beside the big gelding and patted its gleaming neck.

"I thought you were going to turn him out into the paddock," she said, savoring the moment.

"I changed my mind. It's going to bucket down rain any minute. Hey, you're really not afraid, are you?" The Mountie still standing at the horse's head, affectionately scratching its nose, was mildly surprised. "Most people find the boy a bit intimidating close up."

"I respect his superior strength and size," she replied, her enjoyment of being near the horse becoming obvious in her relaxing attitude. "But I don't fear him. He'd know if I did and probably react in response."

"You seem to know a fair bit about horses," he said, going around to the horse's left side. He threw the stirrup up over the saddle and began to loosen the girth.

"I told you, my father taught me to ride when I was a child," she replied. "It's been a couple of years since I've actually been on a horse but I remember the basics of their handling and care."

"Maybe someday you'd like to take Special for a gallop," he said, pulling the saddle from the horse's back and hanging it over a sawhorse.

Ceilidh caught the saddle pad as it was about to slide onto the floor and hung it upside down over the side of an empty stall to dry.

"Would you let me?" she asked, genuinely surprised and delighted. His offer lifted her gloom, and she ran an appreciative gaze and hand over the horse's shining body.

"Certainly," he replied. "He's reliable and smooth as a rocking chair. He's a great horse. I'm glad he didn't pass muster for the musical ride and I got a chance to buy him.''

''Didn't pass muster?'' Ceilidh was amazed and watched as Al began to rub the horse down. ''Why? He's beautiful.''

''But not quite high enough or black enough.'' The Mountie shrugged. ''The RCMP is exacting in its equine recruits.''

''And its human ones as well,'' Ceilidh murmured absently, leaning back against the barn wall.

''You seem to know a fair bit about the RCMP too.'' He paused in his work and turned questioningly toward her.

''Yes, well . . .'' She didn't want to continue the trend the conversation had taken. She pushed away from the wall and brushed hay and dust from her skirt. ''I think I'll go up to the house and make some coffee.''

''That sounds good.'' Al flashed her a gleaming smile. ''You wouldn't have a cup to spare for a fellow horse fancier?''

''Not exactly shy, are you?'' Ceilidh tried to sound annoyed but failed.

''Not one of my weaknesses,'' he said. ''So how about it? And don't worry. Remember, it's their man the Mounties always get, not necessarily their woman.''

''You're also incorrigible,'' she said, again attempting annoyance and failing. ''Okay, come in when you've finished with Special.''

''Thank you kindly, ma'am, I will.'' Still grinning smugly, he turned his back on her and bent to pick up one of Special's front hooves.

''By the way.'' She paused as she was about to leave. ''Why did you name him Special? That's an odd name for a horse.''

''Because, although he didn't make it in the Mounties, he had special qualities that appealed to me.''

''Such as?'' Ceilidh pressed inquisitively.

''Heart of gold and bright as a button . . . everything anyone could want in a companion,'' Al replied simply, starting to pick gravel and debris from the horse's iron-clad hoof.

As Ceilidh walked back to the house she was surprised at how much better she felt. Constable Allan Dumont was a thoroughly charming and engaging man, and he had caught her up in his buoyant mood as easily as a feather rises in the wind.

That's all well and good, she thought. *But this is as far as it goes. I won't get any more deeply involved with him than I am right now. I know only too well the pain that comes from loving a Mountie.*

The nineteenth-century farmhouse had been renovated with all modern conveniences but in such a manner that it had lost none of its turn-of-the-century charm. The big homey kitchen into which Ceilidh stepped had a refrigerator, electric stove, dishwasher, and microwave oven along a side wall by a door that led to what had once been a pantry; on the opposite side near a large, newly installed bay window was an oak table and chairs, a potbellied wood stove, an overstuffed couch, and a maple rocking chair. The green gingham window curtains and tablecloth complemented walls papered in Victorian print above a four-foot base of polished oak wainscoting. Ceilidh loved it.

She put water and coffee into a percolator on a counter near the back door and opened a cupboard door in search of anything to serve with it as a snack. *How strange*, she thought, taking a box of chocolate chip cookies off a shelf. *Half an hour ago I was drowning in despair. Now I'm playing tea party with a Mountie!*

She paused. A Mountie, yes, but definitely one of the best-looking ones she'd ever seen. And if, as a book title had once suggested, men were only for dessert, he was definitely baked Alaska. She felt a smile tickling her lips as she took out a sparkling white plate rimmed with a pattern of fresh green leaves and scattered cookies on it.

Then she glanced about to see if the kitchen was tidy and noticed the old guitar leaning against the wainscoting near the wood stove. It must have belonged to a former tenant, she had decided when she had moved in. Now, chuckling as she remembered her attempt to play it one lonely evening last weekend, she picked it up and carried it into the parlor. Even if she did love country music, she wasn't about to become one of its stars she had discovered.

She returned to the kitchen and placed matching coffee cups, sugar bowl, and cream pitcher with the food on the table, then pulled open a drawer in search of cloth napkins. As she placed the neatly ironed squares beside the mugs, the thought crossed her mind that she was acting like a teenager on her first date.

A Mountie is coming for a cup of coffee just this once, she reminded herself sharply. *And we're definitely not going to make a practice of it. I'll make it clear he has open access to the barn and fields but certainly not to the house. It'll be okay. All I have to do is remember he's RCMP.*

At that moment a tap at the door announced his arrival. Ceilidh was forced out of her thoughts.

"Come in," she called, checking the coffee.

"Hello again," he said, stepping inside and closing the door on the rising winds and first spattering drops of rain. "It has the makings of a nasty night. Even Special seems glad to be comfortably nestled in his box stall munching his hay."

He took the chair Ceilidh indicated at the table and picked up a cookie. He bit into it and, for a moment, munched contentedly as he looked about the room.

"This is a great kitchen," he remarked as she poured coffee into his mug. "Keeps its character without any of the former inconveniences.''

''The rest of the house is the same,'' she said, pleased with his appreciation. ''I was delighted when I first saw it. I was a tad leery of what type of accommodation the Department of Education would provide but this is great. The only problem I've had is with the water heater. It's old and, if overtaxed, blows its fuse. But that's a small matter. The rest of the place is wonderful. Even the stable is in excellent repair. In fact, I was toying with the idea of getting a horse myself. It's always been a dream of mine but now . . .''

Memories of optimistic future plans suddenly brought the disappointments of the last five days flooding back over her mind and she paused, stirring her coffee absently.

''But now what?'' He leaned toward her as she sat dejectedly across from him at the table. ''Surely this place hasn't lost its charm for you already?''

''No, it's not the place.'' She tried to keep her tone even, but just then a ragged bolt of lightning cracked open the dark sky. In the ensuing roll of thunder and deluge of pouring rain, her resolve snapped and, her words ragged with pain, she confessed, "It's me. I'm a failure as a teacher."

Unlike heroines in melodramas, however, she didn't burst into tears. She simply sniffed sharply and gazed deeply into her coffee. And unlike heroes in melodramas, Allan Dumont did not leap up and draw her into his manly arms. Instead, he arose, went to the refrigerator, and got a box of Kleenex from its top.

"Here," he said, putting it down without ceremony in front of her. "Blow your nose. Then tell me all about it."

He returned to his chair and picked up his coffee cup. Ceilidh hesitated only a moment before she pulled out a tissue and did as he suggested.

"There's really nothing to say," she said, struggling to keep her voice from cracking. "I'm just not cut out to be a teacher, that's all."

"That's all!" He put down his cup, placed his elbows on the table, and leaned forward, cupping his chin in his hands. "Sounds pretty serious to me. Declaring yourself a failure in a career you've obviously worked long and hard to realize is no small potatoes and definitely warrants serious discussion. Now tell me, why do you see yourself as a failure? Talk, girl.''

Ceilidh blew her nose again and looked out into the rain thundering down to make puddles in the farmyard's long, unpaved driveway. Almost before she knew it, she had poured out her heart about her problems with her students. Without using any names, she told him about the attention-deficit child and the learning disabled student, and climaxed it all with an account of Jason's disruptive behavior and furious departure.

''You've analyzed the first two,'' he said. ''Now give me your ideas on your third anonymous case.''

''Peer pressure, puberty, but mainly a dysfunctional family, I'd wager, from his state of physical neglect.'' She shook her head defeatedly.

''Ummm,'' he said, slowly making a steeple with his fingers. ''Sounds like some excellent diagnostic work, Miss Highland. Hardly the evaluations of someone unable to understand children and their problems.''

''What good is any diagnosis if I can't treat the problem?'' She refused to be comforted and remained staring miserably out into the rain.

"What good is treating any symptoms without first coming to an accurate diagnosis?" he said. "One step at a time, teacher lady."

"Do you really think so?" Ceilidh turned slowly to face him.

"I most definitely do. Think about it over the weekend. Analyze each case separately. And then don't brood over it. Think about your good students too, and how you can help them. You must have some excellent workers among them."

"Of course I do." Ceilidh brightened instantly. "There's Emma Murray. She's only ten but already her writing is showing tremendous promise. And Johnnie Fulbright, a budding computer genius if ever there was one. And Bobbie Myers who eats up math problems like a little Pac-Man, and . . ."

"Well, then." Allan Dumont stood up and grinned. "I see no failure here. Get on with it, girl."

He walked over to the door but paused with his hand on the knob. "I have to go. The kids will be waiting for me."

"Kids?" Ceilidh felt an unpleasant lurch inside at his words. "You have children? You're married?"

"No," he replied. "The kids from your school. I use the school bus to drive them to town on Friday nights for water safety lessons at the aquatic centre. Afterwards we go for pizza. It gives them something to do and they learn valuable lessons. I decided to try the idea early last spring when I discovered that, in spite of their proximity to a large body of water and the fact that they may, like their parents, someday earn a living fishing that water, most of the local kids couldn't swim and hadn't the least idea about water safety or rescue methods. In an area like this, these skills can often mean the difference between life and death."

"So you know them better than I do," she said. "Why did you let me ramble on and on, using anonymous names to disguise their identity?"

"You needed to talk and I wanted your insights," he said. "I want to help these kids too, and I don't have the expertise in child psychology and learning disabilities you obviously do."

''And how did my learned opinions stack up against your months of actual experiences with them?'' she asked.

''Matched to a T,'' he said. ''But now I have labels for their problems and interests and a better comprehension. Thanks.''

He started to leave once more but turned back to her again. ''Don't give up on that horse idea. It would be great to have someone to ride with.'' Then he dashed out into the downpour.

Chapter Three

The following morning dawned bright and clear, everything freshly washed from the recent rain. The maples along the drive leading up to the house, just beginning to change to their autumn hues of red, gold, and orange, beaded droplets from the previous night's deluge still clinging to their brilliant foliage, glistened like jewels in a huge, earth-toned necklace. A light breeze ruffled the grass on the big field in front of the house and sent its clover-scented breath wafting over to the young woman who had just emerged from the front door.

Ceilidh, clad in jeans, her favorite faded

flannel shirt hanging loosely out over them, stepped out onto the front veranda and stretched languidly, happily. She loved this place and after Allan Dumont's pep talk yesterday, she knew she could stay.

She went to the railing, placed her hands on it, and bent forward to draw in a deep breath of the crystalline air. Even a half mile from the bay, she could still catch whiffs of its clear, salty tang. What a great morning for a canter down the lane behind the house, into the trees, and out along the beach, she thought and wondered for a moment if she dared take Special for a run.

She had just decided it was not a good idea, not without Constable Dumont's specific permission, when she saw the Mountie's gray Jeep coming down the highway, a horse trailer in tow. At the farm gate he slowed, turned in, and then drove carefully up the dirt drive still pockmarked with puddles from yesterday's rain. Oh no, she thought with a dart of regret. He'd come to take Special away.

He waved to her as he drove past the house, then continued on down to the barn. Disappointed at losing the opportunity to go riding, Ceilidh went down the steps and followed the trailer to where it had stopped near the stable door.

"Good morning." Allan Dumont jumped out of the vehicle and greeted her cheerfully. "Perfect morning for riding, isn't it?"

He wore jeans, a faded blue chambray shirt, and riding boots and was as devastatingly attractive as she remembered. *Be strong,* she gave herself a mental prod. *Remember exactly what he is.*

"Yes," she said aloud a bit absently and then stopped short a few feet behind the trailer. "There's a horse in there," she said, surprised, then realized how dumb such a statement of the obvious must sound.

"There certainly is." The Mountie came around the vehicle to lower the tailgate. "Her name is Chance. She's a great little liver chestnut, perfect for a lady who needs to learn to take a few . . . chances, that is."

Amazed beyond speech, Ceilidh could only watch as he backed the beautiful little dark brown animal out of the trailer and turned her about for the young woman's inspection.

"She's gorgeous!" Ceilidh went to place a hand on the mare's neck.

"I'm glad you like her," he said, grinning and rubbing the white star on the animal's forehead. "Because she's yours for as long as you wish. I leased her and her equipment for you for an indefinite period beginning today. Now, let's saddle up and go for a gallop down the beach."

"Wait just a minute!" Ceilidh began to protest but he had already handed her Chance's lead rope and headed into the barn to get Special.

Overwhelmed, yet feeling a flood of pleasure envelope her, Ceilidh stood stock-still for a moment. Then she was aroused to action by the mare's velvet nose nuzzling her affectionately.

"Okay, okay," she said and laughed. "He hasn't left us much choice, has he? I'll tie you to the fence while I saddle you. I assume Constable Dumont has also presumed to bring a saddle, pad, and bridle for you."

Twenty minutes later the horses were galloping companionably side by side along the wide expanse of sandy beach below the house. Ceilidh, her chestnut hair whipped back in the wind, was laughing, her face bright with the sheer exhilaration of the pace. She had almost forgotten how much she enjoyed a good canter.

''Race you to that big rock!'' she cried and put her heels to Chance's sides.

''Hey, head start! Not fair!'' he yelled, urging Special after her.

In the short sprint Chance did manage to outdistance the big gelding but Ceilidh knew that in a long run, it would have been no contest. Al and his mount would have been the victors.

She reined to a halt and swung Chance about.

''Okay, we'll give you this one,'' Al said, pulling up beside her. ''But next time Ceilidh Highland, I'll be ready to take you on even though I have to admit you do ride exceptionally well. Some people lack the courage and aggressiveness necessary to handle a horse successfully. But not you. Definitely not you.''

She laughed again in pure delight, pleased at his obvious admiration. ''I'm having a great time,'' she admitted. ''But we'd better cool these horses down. I have to get back. I have a ton of laundry to do and multiple lessons to organize. I also want to prepare a few meals I can put in the freezer and use as easy suppers during the week.''

''Meals? Genuine home cooking?'' He brought Special in step with Chance as they started at a trot up the trail that led back to the farmhouse. ''I haven't had a good home-cooked meal in ages.''

''Do you live alone?'' Ceilidh was suddenly aware of how little she knew about Constable Allan Dumont.

''I live with Corporal Harry Aimes in a house that doubles as the RCMP headquarters for this area,'' he said. ''And normally his wife, Susan, cooks for us. She's expecting a baby soon, however, and has gone to visit her mother for a few weeks before the big event. Harry is a great guy but his idea of three meals a day doesn't extend much beyond scrambled eggs. At the rate we're consuming them, every chicken within a fifteen-mile radius will be throwing up their wings in despair of supplying our needs.

''To make matters worse, Harry promised Susan he would keep her kitchen in pristine condition so he absolutely refuses to let me inside. I can't prepare anything for myself even if I had the time . . . which I usually don't. With only two of us policing this area, we're generally either on duty or on call.''

''This is the point where I'm supposed to take pity on you and invite you to dinner some evening, right?'' Ceilidh glanced over at him in a pretense of annoyance.

''Well . . . yes.''

''Well, in that case and in view of the fact that you are responsible for getting me this wonderful mare, what are you doing for dinner tonight?''

''Luckily, not a thing. And I'm not on duty tonight either so I won't have to leave right afterwards . . . if you don't want me to.'' His eyes twinkled wickedly.

''Don't press your welcome, Constable,'' she retorted and nudged Chance into a faster trot.

''Don't worry, ma'am. Thank you kindly, ma'am.'' His brown eyes were mischievously teasing, inviting a fun-filled rebuttal. She ignored him.

She definitely wasn't worried. She was immune to his charm. He would discover the fact for himself that evening, she decided.

Several hours later Ceilidh ran a brush through her shoulder-length chestnut hair and was pleased with its body, bounce, and sheen. Her new lipstick seemed just the right shade too, she thought, leaning into her mirror. She only wished she felt as confident about the ankle-length cotton skirt in autumn hues of bronze, gold, and amber that draped smoothly over her slim hips and coordinated with the tangerine-colored, short-sleeved top.

For the third time she adjusted the simple gold chain that hung in the blouse's oval opening at her throat. Was it appropriate? Or would it look out of place with her casual attire? She'd wear it anyway, she decided. It would serve as a reminder of why she must not get involved with handsome, thoroughly appealing Constable Allan Dumont.

Her father, Sergeant John Highland of the Royal Canadian Mounted Police, had given it to her when she had graduated from high school. It was one of her most treasured possessions. She loved both her parents but she and her father had had the close relationship of kindred spirits. He had taught her to ride over her mother's protests and fears and their time together with horses had cast a special bond between them.

Until his retirement from the force three years ago, Ceilidh had constantly worried about his safety. Each time he had been late coming home from work or when she heard of a police officer being killed or injured in the line of duty, Ceilidh had felt her fears rising to fever pitch.

One night shortly after Ceilidh had entered her final year in high school, her nightmares had been realized. The call had come informing her and her mother that Sergeant Highland had been seriously wounded in the line of duty.

Ceilidh would never forget that terrible drive to the hospital beside her mother. Marcia Highland's hands had been white knuckled on the steering wheel, her lovely face taut and grim.

At the hospital they had found John Highland lying horribly still and near death in the intensive care unit amid a seemingly incomprehensible tangle of tubes and equipment. Ceilidh had watched, mute and frozen with fear, as her mother had drawn a chair close to the bed, taken her husband's hand, and spoken softly and reassuringly to the unconscious man.

"You'll be fine, Jack," Marcia Highland had murmured. "You saved a life tonight. You'd do no less if you had it to do all over again. I'm proud, so very proud of you."

There had not been the slightest hint of her own fear or distress. Ceilidh had never admired her mother more than at that moment. She was certain she could never behave so wonderfully, so serenely. Therefore, she could never get involved with a Mountie.

Now she let the chain fall from her fingers, struggled back to the present, and stared at her image in the mirror. All that had been years ago. Right now her concern must be about the evening ahead and how she dressed for it.

Turning from side to side, she returned to her internal debate about her outfit. Maybe the whole look was wrong, she fussed. She didn't want to appear to have dressed up to have dinner with Constable Allan Dumont. She didn't want to give him the idea she was trying to make an impression on him, for heaven's sake. But somehow serving dinner to an invited guest in jeans didn't seem right either. . . .

The smell of pot roast broke in on her reflections. She gasped and made a dash downstairs to the kitchen. It wouldn't matter how she was dressed if the dinner was burned to a crisp.

When she placed the roaster on the stovetop and removed its cover, however, she smiled in satisfaction. Meat and vegetables were done to perfection in an appetizing pool of rich brown gravy. Her mother's pot roast recipe always turned out beautifully. She replaced the lid, left the roaster on the stovetop, and bent to place a tray of biscuits and an apple pie in the still-hot oven. Then she went to set the table.

Although she was still in doubt about her appearance, she had no qualms about the meal. There definitely was nothing suggestive of an intimate evening in pot roast, biscuits, and apple pie. She was glad she had stifled her initial thought of beef bourguignon, Caesar salad, and cheesecake. That definitely was a recipe for romance.

As she put the finishing touches on the

table she wondered if she should include wineglasses. Al might bring a bottle. Dinner guests usually did bring wine. But, then, what if he didn't? She didn't have a drop in the house. She'd look ridiculous putting out glasses with nothing to fill them. No wineglasses, then. She would just wait and see.

She stepped back and surveyed the place settings critically. The sparkling green-and-white dishes looked just right with the hunter green place mats and napkins. The flatware gleamed in contrast to the soft glow of the polished oak table. She felt a warm feeling of anticipation suddenly wash over her and was annoyed. It's only supper with a riding buddy, she told herself, turning away. No occasion for feeling all cozy and domestic.

She was taking the biscuits out of the oven when a knock sounded at the door.

''Come in,'' she called.

''Hey, something smells wonderful!'' Al, in tan bush pants and beige safari shirt, stepped into the kitchen and Ceilidh nearly breathed an audible sigh of relief. He definitely wasn't dressed for a date. In his hand he carried a bottle labeled "Home-made Apple Cider."

Ceilidh nearly laughed aloud as her fears of having to avert any romantic notions Al might be harboring fled. He wasn't any more interested in getting involved with her than she was with him. Great! Now they could get on with simply enjoying their friendship.

"I bought this at a fund-raiser some of the local ladies organized last month," he said, grinning, and handed the bottle to her. "And until now, I wasn't sure what I would do with it. The lady who sold it to me went to great pains to explain it was completely nonalcoholic. I think she was afraid of being guilty of selling illicit liquor to a member of the local constabulary. Would you like to try it?"

"Why not?" Ceilidh took the bottle and headed for the cupboard to open it. "No one I know has ever been seduced on apple cider."

"Really? That's disappointing news." He was grinning after her wickedly. "Hey, these look great!"

He picked up one of the fresh-from-the-oven biscuits and dropped it instantly.

''Ow! Hot!''

''Don't be in such a hurry!'' she said. ''Take a seat and I'll pop the cork.'' She held up the bottle. ''One step at a time, Constable.''

During dinner they talked companionably about their mutual love of horses until, along that course, Al brought the conversation around to families.

''I kept Special at my parents' farm in Quebec's Eastern Townships until I moved here,'' he said. ''Although they weren't thrilled with the idea at first, Dad and Mom really missed the big clown when I took him away.''

''Your parents live on a farm in Quebec?'' Ceilidh asked, more curious than she cared to admit to know more about Constable Allen Dumont.

''Hobby farm,'' he elaborated. ''Dad's retired from a career as a public defender; Mom, from her job as a social worker.''

''You never considered following either of their careers?'' she asked, thinking how much more acceptable he would have been in either of those professions.

''Actually, I did.'' He leaned back in his chair, relaxed and entirely too attractive for

Ceilidh's liking. ''I studied law and even passed the bar exams. I was only in a barrister's office a month, however, when I knew that it wasn't the life for me. I wanted to help people but I needed to be out in the field, at the grassroots level. I resigned and within a month had been accepted into the RCMP.''

''But you could still go back into a career as an attorney.'' Ceilidh was hopefully picturing him safely seated behind a wide mahogany desk in a three-piece suit and reading glasses, studiously going over briefs.

''Yes, but I won't,'' he said and the determination in his brown eyes told her he meant it. ''I like what I do . . . I've found my place in helping people in trouble. It's where I'll stay.''

''But the risks, the danger . . .'' Ceilidh was becoming vehement and she had to stop herself.

''Life is risky from its beginning.'' He shrugged. ''The only difference is that I've been trained to evaluate the danger in any given situation and react in the most effective way. As a result, I'm probably safer than most people.''

''I don't agree,'' Ceilidh said, shaking her head.

''Well, then, let's agree to disagree about my career.'' He lightened the tone of their conversation suddenly. ''Now tell me about your folks. And how they came to give you that lovely, unusual name. Are they teachers too?''

''No.'' Ceilidh spoke slowly weighing her words carefully. ''They're retired and living a five-hour drive from here in Saint Andrews–by-the-Sea. Dad's pursuing his lifelong passion for photography and Mom, a retired pediatrics nurse, is finally getting a chance to paint. The Fundy coast is perfect for both of their interests and they're very happy.''

''Good,'' he said. ''I like to hear about happy couples. I hope to be half of one someday myself. Now tell me how you came by that remarkable name.''

''It's Gaelic.'' Ceilidh could barely keep the relief out of her voice as he failed to continue questioning her about her parents. The last thing she wanted him to know was about her father and her fears for him. ''My mother is Scottish. She chose it. It means a party with friends and song and dance and while it's spelled Ceilidh, it's pronounced 'Kaylee.' She felt it went perfectly with our family name Highland.''

''It's a beautiful name,'' he said softly. ''And it suits. You're a party with song and dance, if ever I met saw one, Ceilidh Highland.''

Ceilidh looked over at him and thought how wonderful his brown eyes were when they were soft with caring and interest, how broad his shoulders were as he leaned toward her, how wonderfully appealing all his features were. . . .

''Dessert?'' she asked, rising abruptly. She had to get out of this moment while she still could.

''That was a great meal,'' Al commented a few minutes later as he finished helping Ceilidh put their dessert plates into the dishwasher and straightened up to flash her a smile that would have lit up any movie screen and most women's hearts. Ceilidh was chagrined to discover she was no exception and turned quickly away to put the roaster to soak in the sink.

''Coffee on the veranda?'' she asked, indicating cups and percolator on the sideboard. "It's a nice evening, too cool for mosquitoes and blackflies but still warm enough to be outside."

"Good idea," he said. "I'll get a tray."

"No, no," she protested jokingly. "You brought the cider; I'll bring you the coffee. Go out and take a seat on the hammock."

"As you wish." He grinned. "Who am I to fight man's primeval right to be attended by a beautiful serving wench?"

"Get!" Ceilidh caught his bantering mood and pointed toward the front door. "Get or you'll find out what it's like to be severely disciplined by aforesaid serving wench!"

When she joined him a few minutes later she found him sitting in the hammock on the front veranda idly strumming "Rocky Mountain High" on the guitar he must have taken from the parlor on his way to the front veranda.

"John Denver fan?" she asked, putting the tray down on a small table near the railing.

"Country music in general," he replied, looking over at her and giving her an unbidden quickening of the pulses. He was almost overwhelmingly attractive sitting in the hammock, relaxed and strumming that old guitar. She had to remind herself sharply that he was an RCMP officer and totally unacceptable for anything beyond the most casual friendship.

''What about you?'' he asked after a pause.

''I'm not sure I'd want my students to know . . . I'm trying to give them at least a passing appreciation of Mozart and his buddies . . . but I love the stuff. Play on, McDuff.''

With a chuckle Ceilidh curled up on the opposite end of the hammock to listen.

''I'm not very good,'' he said with a shyness that surprised and delighted Ceilidh.

''That's okay,'' she said, settling herself comfortably, her colorful skirt spread out about her. ''I'm not a very critical listener.''

Soon he had pulled her into his impromptu recital. Ceilidh found herself happily singing along with him, finally ending with a raucous version of the current number-one country hit.

When they finally stopped, laughing and breathless, Ceilidh realized she was having a wonderful time. Constable Allan Dumont was great fun and she wanted to go on and on enjoying his company.

"That was terrific." Al leaned forward and placed the guitar against the porch railing. "But now I really have to go. I'm on duty at midnight."

They had been having such a good time, Ceilidh hadn't noticed how late it had grown. Across the highway, a slice of moon was rising over the pines. From the ditch along the road, frogs were raising their voices in song. The air was fragrant with a mix of clover, pine, and the earthy pungency of a nearby farmer's freshly plowed field. The magic of a country night enveloped the couple on the old-fashioned gingerbread trimmed farmhouse veranda in warm, silky darkness. Ceilidh felt a shiver of excitement pass over her as Al arose, then paused to look down at her. Suddenly she felt as breathless as the calm evening; butterflies danced around her heart.

"I'll take care of the horses tomorrow," she heard herself saying distantly in a vain effort to keep the moment prosaic. "You can return the favor someday when I'm busy."

"Well, thanks." He held out a hand to help her up from the hammock. Reflexively she accepted.

Her reaction was equally reflexive but totally unexpected. The moment his warm, brown fingers closed over her cold ones, she felt an instant magic racing through her body. *No!* she cried inwardly and wrenched away from him the moment she was on her feet.

"Sorry," he said. "Did I hurt you?"

"No . . . no," she stuttered, "it's okay."

"I'll go then," he said and started for the front steps.

She followed him absently and paused at the top as he started to descend. On the first step, however, he turned and gently took Ceilidh by both arms. His lower position brought them nearly face-to-face. Ceilidh knew she should try to get away but couldn't summon either the strength or the courage to do it.

"Good night, Ceilidh," he said softly, his tone as sensuous as a caress. "It's been a great evening." He leaned forward and kissed her lightly on the forehead. "Pleasant dreams, little party friend."

With that he turned, stuffed his hands

into his pockets, and, whistling in the darkness, headed for his Jeep. Ceilidh was left leaning weakly against the porch post, the memory of warm fingers and gentle lips sapping her strength.

Chapter Four

The day Ceilidh Highland met the man of her dreams began with the ringing of the telephone. She had been lost in a nightmare in which she had been riding on the beach with Al. She had been outdistancing him on Chance when suddenly a shot had rung out. She had whirled just in time to see Al, resplendent in RCMP red serge, toppling from Special. He was clutching his chest.

Her eyes flew open and she sat bolt upright in bed. No, no, no she cried in her heart. Then, becoming aware of the unreality of her horror, she gave herself a sharp mental reprimand, struggled into a semblance of self-control, and lifted the receiver.

"Hello," she said and was startled at the shakiness in her voice.

"Ceilidh? Are you all right?" Karen Blackwell's tone was concerned.

"Fine, just fine, thank you, Mrs. Blackwell." Ceilidh pulled herself up on her pillows, instantly fully awake.

"Good." Her supervisor's voice sounded confidently relieved. "I'm sorry to be calling so early but I received the request late yesterday and was only able to verify everything this morning. I did, however, want to give you as much time as possible to prepare."

"Prepare?" Ceilidh was becoming suspiciously apprehensive. "For what, Mrs. Blackwell?"

"For Neville Brinkley's visit," she said. "He's an associate professor of education at the University of New Brunswick currently working on a thesis about one-teacher schools, past and present. He's requested permission to observe you and your facilities for a few days." Goodness! Ceilidh felt her heart skip a beat. *I can't be hearing correctly.* She tapped the receiver sharply to make certain it was transmitting properly.

"I wasn't in agreement," she heard Mrs. Blackwell continuing. "You need time to accustom yourself . . . but the department was adamant and with their investment in the project I couldn't refuse. He'll be arriving later today. I'm really sorry, Ceilidh."

"I understand," Ceilidh replied calmly but inside she had suddenly turned to jelly. This is just what she needed, being forced under a microscope at this stage of her work. There was no way to refuse, however.

Ceilidh spent the morning and early afternoon in a frenzy of housecleaning and lesson preparation. She hurried through the stable work and was glad Al was on duty until at least noon. She couldn't deal with him right now.

In the turmoil of activity, Ceilidh wondered what sort of man Neville Brinkley would be. His name suggested a short, balding, middle-aged gentleman with thick glasses and a tendency toward absentmindedness. Oh, well, she told herself he could at least act as a buffer between her and Constable Dumont. Last night had shown her she could use all the help she could get against the Mountie's charm. Even if Al didn't have the qualifications necessary to become her someone special, he was exerting a disturbing influence in her life she didn't need right now.

At four o'clock a red sports car turned into the farm driveway. Ceilidh started for the door, stopped, started again, then decided to wait for a knock. Rushing out to meet Professor Brinkley would make her look nervous. She mustn't look as if she were a quaking mass of hypertension. She brushed a fleck from her tan dress pants, hoped her linen blouse and new pumps coordinated with them, and patted her hair into place.

The moment she saw Neville Brinkley, however, all previous uncertainties dissolved into one positive. He was definitely someone special. Tall, blond, blue-eyed, and wonderfully attractive with a permanently thoughtful expression, stylish glasses on the bridge of his straight, perfect nose, he fairly exuded the security of academia combined with a physical appeal at once subtle and yet definitely undeniable.

Ceilidh would have bet her job that he

wore a cardigan on cool evenings and that his feet had never known riding boots or dusty sneakers like those of some people she knew. She was delighted.

''Miss Highland?'' He stood on the doorstep and extended a nicely manicured hand. ''I'm Neville Brinkley. Your supervisor told you I was coming, I believe?''

''Yes, of course.'' She smiled, accepted his offer, and spoke a bit too eagerly. ''Won't you come in, Professor?''

She glanced at the sleek red sports car parked in the yard behind him. Its presence added to her pleasure. Solid but not stodgy, she thought. Great!

''I'll just get my bags,'' he said and turned to go back to the car.

''Let me help,'' she said and followed his broad Harris tweed–covered shoulders down the walk to the car.

He had barely cracked the trunk and was walking around to the rear of the vehicle when Ceilidh's attention was drawn by the sound of another vehicle approaching. Turning, she was chagrined to see Al's muddy Jeep careening into the yard. The Mountie braked to a halt close behind the gleaming Toyota and jumped out.

"Hi, Cail," he called, sauntering leisurely over to join them on long, jean-clad legs and dusty Reeboks. His faded denim shirt was open at the throat, revealing a hard, tanned chest. "Company?"

Neville Brinkley turned from pulling a pristine Samsonite suitbag from the trunk and faced the other man squarely.

"Well . . ." Al was visibly taken aback.

"Neville Brinkley, associate professor from the University of New Brunswick," the tall blond man was quick to introduce himself. "I'll be observing Miss Highland at her work for a few days. And you are?" He smiled and extended his hand.

"Allan Dumont, local RCMP," Al said, his eyes narrowing as he slowly accepted the other man's greeting. "Exactly how long will this observing take, *Neville*?"

He's jealous, Ceilidh thought in surprise. *We hardly know each other and yet he's jealous! It's ridiculous.*

Yet somewhere deep inside, although she was loath to admit it, Ceilidh Highland was flattered and delighted. Al, for all his inappropriateness for the role of man of her dreams, was an exciting, wonderfully handsome man, perfect for that position in almost any other woman's life; any other woman who would wildly envy Ceilidh her ability to incite his jealousy.

"As long as my research requires," Neville Brinkley said pleasantly, ignoring the Mountie's abruptness. "Do you work around here, Sergeant?"

"Constable," Al corrected, annoyance coloring his tone as he stepped forward to pull a second valise from the trunk. "And yes, I do. Now let's get you settled in. The sooner you get to work, the sooner you can get back home to the little woman."

"I appreciate your concern, Constable." Neville Brinkley's tone remained unflinchingly cordial. "But there is no little woman at home. Actually, as I was driving down here today I was thinking what a delightful view of the coast this area had and how fortunate I am to be working here. The longer I'm here, the better, as far as I'm concerned."

"Yeah, well . . ." Al hefted two bags and started toward the house. "Let's get on with it then."

"Professor Brinkley, I'm sorry," Ceilidh apologized as soon as the Mountie had disappeared into the kitchen. She felt herself beginning to burn with anger and embarrassment and was no longer pleased with Al's apparent jealousy of her companion. "Constable Dumont keeps his horse in the barn. When he spends time here, he's generally at the stable or off riding somewhere. You won't have to encounter him often."

"Don't concern yourself, Miss Highland." He turned to her and smiled. "I was once a middle-school teacher. I'm accustomed to rude adolescents."

Wow! Ceilidh thought. *How could anyone possibly be rude to anyone who looks like that when he smiles.*

She and the professor followed Al into the house where the Mountie deposited the luggage he had been carrying unceremoniously in a heap in the middle of the kitchen floor. Then, a scowl etched across his handsome face, Constable Allan Dumont left with a supposedly accidental slam of the screen door.

"Come through the parlor, Professor Brinkley," Ceilidh said, trying to ignore Al's inhospitable behavior. "I'll show you upstairs and you can decide which bedroom will best meet your needs."

At the top of the stairs Ceilidh paused

and opened the door to the large master bedroom to her left.

"I'm settled in the smaller room across the hall," she said. "And the one at the rear of the house is really little more than a big closet with a bed, nightstand, and dresser. This is probably the best choice for you."

"I do like its airiness," he said, advancing inside and putting one of his suitcases on the wide, old-fashioned, quilt-covered brass bed. "Two big windows, one overlooking the front veranda and other with an excellent view of that road over there. Where does it lead, by the way?"

"To the wharf where most of the local fishermen tie up their boats," she said. "It's a dirt road and quite dusty at times. Consequently, I'm afraid you may not be able to open the window on that side of the room very often. Actually, it sticks. I guess it hasn't been used much because of that particular problem."

"This one works beautifully," he said.

He had gone to the tall, old-fashioned window overlooking the front veranda and slid it up and wide open. "I like to sleep with my bedroom window open, weather permitting. I hope you don't mind.''

''That's no problem.'' She smiled, glad to have found something they had in common. ''I like fresh air at night too.'' She turned to leave. ''I'll let you get settled in. If there's anything I can do to help, please let me know.'' She smiled again and left the room.

The moment the door closed behind her, however, her smile vanished. Lips set in a grim, hard line, Ceilidh Highland pushed up the sleeves of her peach-colored blouse and headed toward the stable. She had a few things to say to a certain RCMP constable.

''And just exactly what did you think you were doing back at the house?'' she demanded, swooping into the barn like an avenging angel. Arms akimbo, she confronted Constable Allan Dumont. The Mountie had been rubbing Special down as the big gelding stood in crossties outside his stall but halted at her outburst.

''What?'' He looked at her across the horse's powerful shoulders in apparent complete innocence. His handsome face was as blank as a fresh sheet.

''Don't 'what' me!'' she cried with such vehemence Special snorted and threw up his head. ''You know exactly what I'm talking about! You were barely civil to Professor Brinkley. He's a gentleman, not one of the criminal types you're accustomed to dealing with. I'd appreciate it if you behaved accordingly!''

''That guy is about as much a gentleman as I'm a ballerina,'' he muttered, bending to examine one of Special's front hooves. ''Anyway, I don't see where I did or said anything terribly wrong.''

''Ooooh!'' Ceilidh had reached the end of her patience. One desert tan pump shot out and connected squarely with Constable Allan Dumont's nicely shaped posterior. From being bent over his horse's hoof, the Mountie was sent sprawling headlong into the tangle of straw and manure in Special's box stall.

''Hey!'' he yelled as he landed but Ceilidh was already stomping off toward the house. *Blast Constable Allan Dumont!* she thought over and over again. *Blast him, blast him, blast him!*

Still seething, Ceilidh entered the farmhouse and flung herself down on the couch in the kitchen. Last night she had wanted to be friends with Al, had believed they were well along the road to that destination. Then he had kissed her ever so gently, so unprovocatively, and she had felt that plan shatter into a magical spray of glittering sensations. And today, just when she had met someone who seemed perfectly capable of getting her back on the road toward her dream man, he had again burst through her plans, only this time in a definitely unbidden and totally exasperating manner.

This does it, she thought, angrily punching a pillow. *Constable Allan Dumont, you are out of my life forever!*

"Hello."

Ceilidh started at the sound of his voice and turned to see Neville Brinkley smiling at her from the doorway leading to the parlor.

"Hello." Ceilidh pushed thoughts of Allan Dumont aside and smiled in return. "Have you gotten settled in? Is there any way I can help?"

"I'm fine, thank you, in spite of the fact this place is hardly the Ritz," he said. "I do appreciate the fact that I am invading your privacy, not to mention your working time. I'll try not be be any more of an impediment to you than absolutely necessary.''

He ended with such an apologetic smile that Ceilidh almost completely forgave him his unfavorable delineation of her home.

''I'm sure I'll enjoy working with you,'' she replied, sitting up straight and regaining her composure.

''Nevertheless, I'm grateful for your agreeing to take me on. To show my appreciation I'd like to take you out to dinner this evening. I've been told there's a rather nice seafood restaurant a few miles downshore from here, farther out along the bay. Will you be my guest?''

Surprised by his invitation, Ceilidh did not reply immediately.

''Of course, if you'd prefer to wait until we're better acquainted . . .'' he continued, taking her hesitation for reluctance.

''Oh, no, no . . .'' Ceilidh was suddenly stumbling and completely annoyed with herself. *Along comes this perfectly ideal guy and you turn into a blithering idiot,* a little voice inside scolded her harshly. *Get a grip, girl, or give up. No wonder you've never found Mr. Special.*

"Maybe you already have plans?"

"No, I don't," Ceilidh pulled herself mentally together and arose. "I'd like to go to dinner with you, Professor Brinkley."

"Neville," He smiled again and Ceilidh thought how good some men—tall, handsome, blond men—could look in glasses, Harris tweed, and jeans.

"Neville," she said softly. Then sprucing up her tone, she continued, "I'll just run upstairs and change."

An hour later they were seated at the table Neville had requested overlooking the mouth of the bay. Ceilidh felt mature and sophisticated in her burgundy suit and the gold earrings that matched her father's gift chain. As they discussed their educational backgrounds and future professional plans over seafood chowder, lobster thermidor, and a bottle of white wine, she hoped it was genuine interest she suspected she saw in Neville Brinkley's clear blue eyes.

They were deep in a discussion of Madeline Hunter's mastery teaching strategies by the time the praline cheesecake and coffee arrived. The sun was setting and after the waiter had served their dessert, he hastened to light the candle in the center of the table.

Over the water the sky had turned to tender hues of pink, blue, and gold. The bay, grown still in the last moments of daylight, caught these gentle colors and held them tenderly against its smooth surface. Lulled by fine food and wine and the mellowing of the late summer's day, Ceilidh looked over at Neville Brinkley and found him totally perfect. She smiled contentedly. At last she had found her someone special.

''Would you think I was out of line if I told you you're especially beautiful by candlelight?'' He startled her with his unexpected remark. They were his first words since they had ended their discussion of teaching techniques a few moments earlier and seemed to come from nowhere.

''That's very kind of you.'' Ceilidh tried desperately to think cool and sophisticated, cool and sophisticated but her heart and mind had gone hurtling head over heels at his words.

''It wasn't meant to be kind,'' he said huskily. ''It was an honest, completely objective observation.'' His tone, however, belied his words.

"Then, thank you." Ceilidh knew she couldn't maintain her unruffled facade much longer and deliberately turned the direction of their conversation. "Isn't the sunset beautiful?" she continued, moving in her chair to look out over the rapidly darkening bay. "Look, there's an almost full moon rising."

"Yes, it is," he said, following her lead and turning to look out over the bay. "The scenery all along this coast intrigues me. In fact, I'd like to take a walk along the beach after dinner. Would you come with me? It's a beautiful evening."

A romantic candlelit dinner and now a stroll along a gorgeous stretch of beach in the moonlight with a handsome, perfect-in-every-way man. *I'm in heaven,* Ceilidh thought a few minutes later as she waited for Neville to pay the bill.

But if she were in heaven, why did pot roast and apple pie and teasing brown eyes suddenly dart across her mind?

Chapter Five

The next morning Ceilidh awoke to the smell of fresh coffee and something intriguing toasting. When she went downstairs, showered, and dressed in a bronze-colored linen dress, she found Neville Brinkley absorbed in a book as he sat at the kitchen table, which was set for breakfast for two.

"Good morning," he smiled and arose. "I took the liberty of making a bit of breakfast. English muffins, juice, cereal, and coffee . . . I hope you like it."

"Yes, thank you." Ceilidh accepted the

chair he drew out for her and sat down. "You must have been up early."

"I was," he said, pouring her coffee. "Actually, I've already been for a walk along the beach. Wonderful view, wonderful air."

He popped a split English muffin into the toaster and sat down opposite her as she poured a strange-looking concoction of dried fruits and grains from the box on the table into her bowl.

"It's a new high-fiber, low-fat cereal I brought with me," he said in answer to her unspoken question. "Very nutritious. I hope you'll enjoy it."

"I'm sure I will." Ceilidh shot him a quick smile before returning her attention to the unusual tangle in her bowl and feeling doubtful.

"Ceilidh, I really enjoyed last night," he continued, his tone softening. "In fact, I can't remember when I last had such a delightful evening."

"I had a nice time too, Neville," she replied. She took a sip of her orange juice and hoped she wasn't blushing. His polite correctness made her feel like an awkward schoolgirl with a teacher on whom she had a gigantic crush.

''Perhaps we could take another stroll this evening,'' he said. ''Just a brief walk . . . I know you have a good deal of preparation to do but a few minutes in fresh air prior to academic concentration can have beneficial effects, I've discovered.''

''Yes,'' she said. ''I agree. About six o'clock, then?''

''Excellent,'' he said and arose, taking his book with him. ''I'll be a bit late getting to school this morning. I have some reading to finish. I hope you don't mind if I arrive around ten-thirty?''

''Of course not,'' she replied and smiled up at him. ''It will give me time to get the children settled to their studies.'' Jason in particular, she thought.

''Then it will work to both our advantages,'' he said. ''I'll join you in a few hours.''

He put the two halves of the muffin that had just popped from the toaster on a plate, placed it before her, smiled warmly, and left to go back upstairs.

There goes a true gentleman, Ceilidh thought, buttering the muffin. *Now if I can just keep the children from totally destroying any claim I may have to professionalism, perhaps he'll continue to enjoy my company.*

Trying to formulate a strategy that would serve to satisfy her students' needs and at the same time produce a favorable impression on Neville Brinkley, she was lost in thought as she pulled into the schoolyard a half hour later. She was startled out of her reflections by the sight of an RCMP cruiser parked near the main entrance. As she stopped her car and got out, Al emerged from the police vehicle and waved to her.

"Good morning," he said and Ceilidh felt her breath catch in her throat. If she had previously found him handsome, he was now, in uniform, the superlative of that adjective. Impeccably groomed, his uniform perfectly fitted and pressed, he looked even taller and more broad shouldered than ever. Ceilidh found herself speechless with admiration. For a moment she stared in awe.

"Good morning," he repeated, snapping her out of her trance. "Are you okay? You look as if you'd seen a ghost."

''Good morning,'' she replied unevenly, thinking, *Maybe I have . . . Dad's ghost.*

''I tried to call you last night,'' he said. ''But there was no answer. I considered driving over but then decided I had no good reason to show up at nine-thirty P.M.''

''Neville . . . Professor Brinkley took me out to dinner,'' she replied, recovering herself.

''Until nine-thirty?'' he asked, raising an eyebrow skeptically.

''We went for a walk on the beach later,'' she said, recalling their chaste, shoptalk stroll along the moon-glazed shore and Neville's shy, boyish, innocuous good-night, which she had found completely charming later in the farmhouse kitchen.

''Really?'' Al's handsome face hardened beneath the peak of his police hat. ''And just exactly what happened on this makeout stroll?''

''Makeout stroll!'' Ceilidh's admiration vanished as her full-blown ire returned. ''How dare you imply . . . !''

''Ceilidh, Ceilidh, listen! I'm sorry! That comment was definitely out of line.'' Al was instantly apologetic. ''It's just that I care about you, and I'm worried about you and that Neville Brinkley character being alone in that house together. Please promise me you'll be careful where he's concerned.''

About to retort angrily, Ceilidh was stopped by the honest concern in his words and tone. She looked up into his face and saw sincere caring reflected there.

''Al, I appreciate your interest,'' she said quietly. ''But I'm a big girl. After four years at a coed university, I think I've learned to handle most overly aggressive men.'' She reached out and patted his arm affectionately. ''Please rest assured I'll be just fine.''

She started up the front steps of the school, then paused, turned, and smiled back at him.

''But thanks, Constable. It's nice to know I have a friend who really cares.''

Then she inserted the key in the lock, opened the door, and vanished into the school before he could reply.

Ceilidh was in for another surprise shortly. In class she found a miraculously subdued Jason. He spoke, albeit in a mutter, when she addressed him and generally followed her instructions, albeit grudg-

ingly. She was elated. She didn't understand the teenager's change, but then who
was she to look a gift horse in the mouth?

The analogy made her flinch. It brought
first Chance and then Al to mind. The sin-
cerity of his concern for her had touched
her deeply, had made her feel sheepish as
she recalled her unladylike behavior toward
him in the stable the previous afternoon. If
only he weren't a Mountie . . .

"Miss? Is this right?" Jason brought her
out of her thoughts as he shoved a soiled
notebook across her desk toward her.

She looked down at the scribbler page,
darkened with eraser marks, and broke into
a smile of pure delight as she saw the cor-
rect method and answer finally achieved.

"Yes, Jason, it certainly is," she said.
"I knew you could do it. I really knew you
could."

She flicked a large, red check mark
across his effort and smiled up at the boy
as she handed the work back to him.

"Constable Al was right about you too,"
he surprised her by replying. "He said
you're prettiest when you smile."

"Just when did he say that?" Ceilidh
heard herself asking in reflexive surprise.

"Friday night when he drove us to town," Jason replied. "He said he found you prettiest when you smiled and he'd be obliged if we all did our work and behaved. That way we'd please you and keep you looking your best . . . for him."

"That was thoughtful of him," she replied, struggling to keep her tone pleasantly even. "Now try the next problem, please. You should have no difficulty with it now that you've mastered the concept."

As Jason returned to his seat, Ceilidh felt wreathed in a quandary. Once again she couldn't decide if she should be furious with Al for making personal remarks to her students or eternally grateful for making Neville's first day in her school a much more manageable experience. Constable Allan Dumont had a talent for keeping her perpetually off balance.

Neville arrived promptly at 10:30 A.M., but left shortly after having lunch with her and the children. He said he had to drive back to town for more research material but, with a knowing look at Ceilidh, said he would be back by six.

At 4:30 P.M. Ceilidh closed the building and headed back to the farm. All in all it had been a good day and she felt light-hearted and happy. To celebrate she would take a quick canter down the beach on Chance, she decided, and hurried into the house to change into jeans, boots, and shirt.

She had barely finished changing when a knock sounded on the back door. Ceilidh opened it to find Al in jeans and a gray sweatshirt standing on the porch. In one hand he held a large suitcase; a garment bag was slung over his shoulder.

''Hi,'' he said, flashing that devastating smile.

''Hi,'' Ceilidh replied blankly, puzzled. ''You're going on a trip?''

''No, I'm moving in.'' He brushed past her, still wearing that resolve-melting expression. ''Which bedroom is still empty?''

''Moving in?'' Ceilidh couldn't believe she had heard correctly. ''No, no, no, I think not!''

She was pursuing him hotly as he continued on through the house to the foot of the stairs. There she caught up to him and clutched his arm.

''Why not?'' He paused and turned to her. ''This is a government-rented facility, isn't it? And I'm a government employee who needs a place to live.''

"You live at the RCMP place!" Ceilidh was inarticulate with anger. ''You live with the Aimeses . . . the couple who are having the baby!''

"And it's because of that expected little one that I have to move out," he explained with aggravating calm. ''Susan arrived back this morning with paint, wallpaper, curtains, and all kinds of other paraphernalia for the baby's room . . . my room until now. She wants to start remodeling right away, so who am I to disturb the dreams of a sweet, little expectant mother?''

"But surely they don't plan to put you out forever?''

"Of course not. A carpenter is busy right now building me my very own apartment in the basement. The only problem is it won't be ready for a couple of weeks. Susan and Harry kindly suggested I could sleep on the living room couch, but why should I when there's a perfectly good government-financed room lying fallow here?''

Whistling merrily, he proceeded upstairs with Ceilidh in hot pursuit.

He glanced into the first bedroom, saw a pink nightgown draped over the end of its four-poster, and winked annoyingly at her. "Not this one, I guess."

"Definitely not!" Ceilidh quickly pulled the door shut.

"What about this one?" He pushed open the door across the hall.

With curtains on both windows drawn fully open, the pristinely neat room was illuminated in a blaze of late-afternoon sunlight. A stack of books on a desk near the window overlooking the front porch were the only items of a personal nature in evidence.

"And not this one either . . . I should have realized . . . with those two big windows," he muttered more to himself than to Ceilidh.

"It's Neville's," Ceilidh said needlessly as he shut the door with a sharp bang.

"Well, since that one's too hot"—he gestured toward Ceilidh's room—"and this one's stone cold, I guess I'll have to be like Goldilocks and find the last one just right."

He opened the door at the end of the corridor.

"This is great," he said, going inside the

tiny cubicle. He tossed his luggage aside and flopped down on the bed, bouncing for a moment as he tested its springiness.

"No, no, no!" Ceilidh cried again. "You can't stay here! It's a closet! There isn't enough room! And what will Neville— Professor Brinkley—say?"

"Who cares?" Al paused in his mattress testing, and all the good humor drained out of his face. "I have as much right here as he does. More, in fact." His tone lightened again. "Since I have a position in this house."

"Position? What possible position could you have in this house?"

"Chaperone." He grinned looking up at her. "You definitely need one with that guy in residence."

"Chaperone?" Ceilidh's reply was an irate gasp of indignation. "Why, you judgmental . . . donkey! Neville Brinkley is an academic, a gentleman, a—"

"A colossal pain," he said to end her description and opened his suitcase to remove a shaving kit. "Which way to the bathroom?"

"Ahhhh!" Ceilidh threw her arms in exasperation and flounced out of the room and back downstairs.

She was vigorously brushing Chance, who was standing quietly in the crossties when Al came out to the barn twenty minutes later. He was wearing riding boots, indicating he was planning to take Special out for a run. Ceilidh had to stifle a strong desire to ask to accompany him. No matter what fun a good canter up the beach beside him would be she wasn't about to let her annoyance at his invasion of her home and her hopes for herself and Neville Brinkley subside.

After a quick glance in her direction, Al proceeded on through the stable without a word. He brought Special out of his stall, saddled him, attached a long lead to his halter, and led him out into the paddock to lunge him as if she weren't there.

Humph! she thought, brushing vigorously. *Big chicken . . . has to take the spark out of that brute before he dares mount up.*

But deep down she knew he was only doing the sensible thing by giving the animal a chance to blow off repressed energy before riding him. Taking any horse fresh from his stall for a canter was inviting trouble and she knew it. Al was right in avoiding unnecessary risks, in observing safety rules, and deep down she grudgingly admired him for it.

She saddled Chance, then, carrying a bridle over her shoulder, she led the animal out into the paddock area, a lunge line attached to the mare's halter. Safety was not something she was about to ignore, either.

She had assumed that Al would be gone out along the trail to the beach by now. She was surprised, therefore, to see him riding Special around the paddock, keeping the big gelding to a perfectly controlled, finely executed lope. Man and horse were moving in a harmony that made the performance appear effortless to the untrained observer, but Ceilidh knew better. She had difficulty not pausing and openly admiring the pair.

Instead, she led Chance to the far end of the fenced area and started her in easy circles at the end of the lunge line. As the well-trained mare responded easily to Ceilidh's commands of walk, trot, and lope the young woman had an opportunity to glance at the horse and rider beyond her. They had paused and then suddenly, to her surprise, launched into a few basic, prancing steps of dressage.

''Whoa!'' Ceilidh was overwhelmed. She had to stop her mare and watch.

''Cute, isn't he?'' Al caught her gaze and grinned. ''Just a few tricks he picked up before I bought him.'' He halted the horse, then cantered him over to join her.

''It takes two,'' she replied, forgetting her previous anger in interest. ''You must have a fair amount of expertise in the discipline yourself.'' She had to struggle to keep admiration out of her tone.

''A bit.'' He dismounted and stood grinning at her. ''Want me to share what little I do know about dressage with you? It's great fun.''

''Well . . .'' Ceilidh desperately wanted to say yes but now she was remembering her anger and annoyance at his moving into the house.

''Come on, let's have some fun.'' Al climbed back into the saddle. ''Since we don't have proper dressage equipment, that's all it can be.''

He smiled down at her and she could only nod and climb back onto Chance.

''Friends again?'' he asked softly as they

walked their horses to the middle of the paddock. "Please?"

He looked at her so appealingly she felt a smile tugging at her lips. He was impossible to stay angry with.

"I suppose." She tried to sound grudging but couldn't. "Now let's get on with it. I have other commitments later."

"I bet," he muttered, his expression hardening. He put his heels to Special's sides and sent the big horse forward at a gallop.

Later they were yelling, urging their mounts faster and faster as they raced abound two barrels Al had found in the barn when, out of the corner of her eye, Ceilidh saw Neville Brinkley striding angrily toward the paddock. At the fence he paused, hands on his hips, and glared in Al's direction.

Ceilidh instantly withdrew from the wild, dust-raising activity and trotted Chance, sweating and dirty, over to the fence where the professor stood. Neville, dressed in a pale blue silk shirt and perfectly pressed gray dress pants, could have easily just stepped from the pages of an elegant men's catalog. Blond hair neatly brushed, shoes gleaming with polish, he made Ceilidh uncomfortably aware of her dusty, bedraggled appearance. Self-consciously she tried to brush a few errant strands of chestnut hair back from her face.

"Hi," she said and smiled at him.

"Hello," he said shortly. "You don't seem ready."

"Ready?"

"For our walk along the beach," he said, annoyance coloring his tone. "I specifically said six o'clock."

"I completely forgot!" Ceilidh gasped. "Neville, I *am* sorry! Wait, please. I'll see if Al will take care of Chance and I'll come with you immediately."

She turned her mare and cantered over to Al.

"Will you cool Chance down and put her away?" she asked. "I know it's an imposition but I *did* promise Neville I'd go walking with him. We were having so much fun I forgot."

"But apparently not enough fun for you to tell him to take a flying leap and stay with me." Al's face had darkened with anger.

"Al, don't be like that!" she implored,

hoping Neville was out of earshot. "You and I are good friends. Let's keep it that way. Don't get angry."

"Go." Al reached out for Chance's reins without dismounting and Ceilidh had no choice but to hand them over. She had already committed herself.

She slid off the mare and, with a last, reproving look at Al, turned and walked away although she knew he was glaring after her.

"Let's go," she said as she drew close to Neville. With a careless gesture she brushed dust and dirt from her jeans.

"Looking like that?" he asked skeptically. "Can't you change into a dress?"

"Well, yes, I suppose," she said, chagrined. "You'll have to give me a few minutes."

"Agreed," he said shortly and Ceilidh, trying to justify his abruptness, hurried off to the house.

When she rejoined the professor on the back porch fifteen minutes later, however, he had changed considerably in his outlook. He smiled as he saw her dressed in a calf-length denim dress, her hair neatly brushed into a gather at the nape of her neck, silver hoop earrings her only jewelry.

"You look wonderful," he said. "I'm sorry if I seemed abrupt over at the field but when I saw you roughhousing with that . . . that *Mountie!* Ceilidh, you must be more discreet! Those men are totally un-scrupulous when it comes to women."

"Not all of them," Ceilidh failed to stop herself from replying reflectively.

"No, perhaps not all," he said. "But the vast majority. Now let's put all Mounties out of mind. It's a beautiful evening, meant to be enjoyed. I thought we might walk down to the wharf and watch the fishing fleet come in. I imagine there's a fair amount of activity around that time."

"All right," she said but couldn't help feeling less than excited at the prospect. Neville's concern for her appearance more than her company had left her with less than a positive feeling about their evening.

During their stroll, however, Neville proved to be so completely attentive, she found her negative feelings waning. He riveted all his attention on her, only once dividing it briefly to speak to some of the fishermen at the wharf. And even then, he was charming, drawing Ceilidh into the men's conversation and beaming proudly at her as she captivated the fishermen with her informed questions and comments on the local economy.

"You're amazing," he breathed into her ear as they turned away and started back up the road. "You conversed as easily with those men as if you were a fisheries expert. They were impressed as was I."

"Just a little background I gathered before coming here to work," she said, warmed by his praise.

"You're as clever as you are attractive," he said, softly beaming at her from behind his glasses.

Ceilidh returned the smile, hoping her delight wasn't as apparent as it felt.

"I thoroughly enjoyed our walk," Neville further pleased Ceilidh with his revelation the moment the couple had arrived back át the house and had seated themselves on the front veranda hammock.

"So did I," she replied softly. "It's refreshing to have an expert to discuss educational theories and practices with."

"I'd hardly call myself an expert," he replied shyly, looking down at his hands clasped in his lap. ''But taking on this thesis project has brought me in contact with some of the latest programs. In actual fact, however, I believe I'm getting more grist for my mill from you than any other source. You're a grassroots original in many of your ideas yet you employ most of the best educational philosophies and thoughts of the day in highly innovative and effective ways. I'm impressed.''

He looked over at her and smiled almost embarrassedly.

''Really?'' Ceilidh felt ready to burst with joy. Such praise from a highly knowledgeable colleague was heady stuff. She felt like butter on a warm muffin, all soft and melting.

''Really,'' he replied softly, looking deeply into her wide-eyed pleasure.

Slowly, hesitatingly, he took her hands in his. Then, looking deep into her eyes, he moved slowly forward and put his lips gently over hers.

Ceilidh stifled a gasp of not unhappy surprise. Neville, mistaking her reaction, instantly drew back, arose, and walked to the end of the veranda where he stood slightly stooped, hands gripping the railing, his back to her, his head lowered between his shoulders.

"I'm sorry," he said hoarsely. "I had no right to do that."

"Neville." Ceilidh arose quickly and went to him. Carefully she placed a hand on his arm. "It's all right. I understand. I . . . I've had a wonderful couple of days too."

Slowly he straightened and turned to face her. "Do you mean that, Ceilidh?" he asked shyly.

"Yes," she breathed and the next instant he was drawing her into his arms, against the sensuous softness of his silk shirt. Ceilidh was breathless with anticipation as Neville's lips drew near hers.

"Anyone seen my deodorant?" A bucket of cold water thrown over Ceilidh could not have been more of an unpleasant shock at that moment than Al's voice.

She whirled out of Neville's embrace to see the Mountie coming out onto the veranda wearing only a daisy-printed towel wrapped about his hips, his dark hair still wet from a shower.

"Not out here!" she hissed, advancing toward him with all the murderous venom of a cobra in her heart. "Definitely not out here!"

"Oh, well." Al shrugged, seated himself on the hammock and smiled sweetly up at her. "Maybe I'll just sit here and air-dry myself for a while. Do you know, that water heater cut out just as I was finishing my shower?"

"I don't care what cut out! Just get into the house!" Ceilidh gave up her last semblance of civility and nearly shouted at him. "What will people passing on the highway think? I'm trying to maintain a position of respect in this community and now here you sit . . . !"

"It's all right, Ceilidh." Neville came to join her. "We all should be going inside. I have a lot of work to do. Besides, it's getting chilly and we definitely wouldn't want Constable Dumont to catch his death of cold, would we?" He finished with a withering look at the Mountie.

He turned and strode into the house. As the screen door slammed behind him, Al arose and gave Ceilidh an especially innocuous smile.

"It *is* getting chilly," he said.

"I could kill you!" Ceilidh sputtered. "I most definitely will kill you!"

"Ah, ah, ah!" He wagged a finger annoyingly in her face. "There are stiff penalties for doing away with a law enforcement officer."

Speechless with anger, Ceilidh flung herself into the house and locked the door behind her.

"Ceilidh, open the door!" Al was clutching his towel and shivering as he banged on the closed panel. "Ceilidh, I'm sorry! Let me in!"

"This house has a back door," she shouted. "Run around there. I'm sure the locals passing on the highway will enjoy seeing Mr. Law and Order dashing across the lawn in a big daisy towel!"

Chapter Six

Ceilidh was happy as she stooped to remove her barn-soiled sneakers on the back
porch before going into the kitchen. Clad
in a baggy gray sweatsuit, her hair scraped
back into an untidy ponytail, she had just
finished tending the horses. Her love of the
animals was such that she even enjoyed the
sometimes heavy, often laborious tasks that
went along with them.

She went inside, washed her hands in the
pantry, and returned to the kitchen, hum-
ming a tune, to pour a cup of coffee from
the pot she had set to perk before she went
down to the stable. Leaning against the

cupboards savoring her first sip, she was gazing out the big kitchen windows into the makings of a gorgeous, sun-bright autumn day when Al's voice made her turn toward the parlor doorway.

"How are our babies this morning?" he asked, coming into the room dressed for duty. He appeared to be totally unaware of how prepossessing he was in full-dress uniform. Ceilidh again had to stop herself from gazing admiringly at him.

"Fine, just fine," she replied but flinched as his holster brushed against her as he reached for an empty cup from the cupboard behind her. A timely reminder of her reason not to get involved with him, she thought and was grateful.

"I really appreciate your agreeing to share the barn work," he said, pouring himself a cup of coffee. "It makes it a lot easier for me on these mornings when I have to be on duty at 7:00 A.M. And on days following nights I've been left to freeze out on the front veranda," he finished, his eyes twinkling wickedly.

"You got exactly what you deserved," she said. "The very idea! Parading yourself around outside in only a towel! And you certainly weren't left to freeze on the front veranda. I left the back door open for you. Cereal?'' She altered her tone and finished with saccharine innocence as she took the box of breakfast food Neville had brought from the cupboard.

''Sounds good.'' Al collected two bowls and spoons and followed her to the table.

They sat down and she tumbled a cupful of cereal into each of the bowls. Al paused and stared down at the mixture.

''What is this stuff?'' he asked, examining it gingerly with his spoon.

''It's very nutritious,'' Ceilidh read the long, European name from the side of the box. ''High fiber, low fat. Very good for you. Neville bought it.''

''Figures,'' Al muttered. ''It looks like roots and twigs.'' He shoved the bowl aside, arose and returned to the cupboards to get another box of cereal and two more bowls. He paused at the refrigerator long enough to add a quart of milk to his collection.

''There,'' he said, a satisfied grin on his face as he sat down again at the table and proceeded to fill the fresh bowls from his box. "Now here's a real breakfast food. Satisfaction and fun all in one package."

"Rice Krispies?" she asked, raising her eyebrows. "Really!"

"Yes, really. My cereal . . . I bought it. You know, it's a lot like you, Miss Highland."

"And just how, in your convoluted reasoning, have you managed to come to that conclusion?"

"Observe." He poised the milk over her bowl. "These Rice Krispies have the potential to be great fun; yet there they lie, dull and dry. Then along comes milk, representing Allan Dumont." He tilted the carton and poured. "And violà! Snap, pop, etc. . . . great fun!"

"Idiot!" she muttered, blushing hotly.

"Good morning." Neville Brinkley's voice was hoarse and rasping as he came into the kitchen in pajamas, calf-length robe, and carpet slippers.

"Neville, are you all right?" Ceilidh was instantly concerned about the professor's health but also fervently hoping he hadn't overheard Al's cereal analogy.

"I'm afraid I caught a cold last evening." He coughed and pulled a handkerchief from the pocket of his robe. ''I couldn't have been dressed warmly enough.'' He covered his mouth and nose and sneezed.

''*You* weren't dressed warmly enough!'' Al scoffed under his breath.

Under the table, Ceilidh's foot shot out and kicked him.

''I won't go to school today,'' Neville continued, pretending not to hear. ''I'll rest this morning and drive into town after lunch to see a doctor. I don't want either of you to catch whatever virus I've contracted.''

''Don't worry about us,'' Ceilidh started to rise solicitously. ''Can I get you anything?''

''No, please go on with your breakfast.'' He waved her back into her chair and glanced disparagingly at the box of Rice Krispies. ''But don't indulge in too much of that kiddie food. Such choices can be detrimental to your future well-being.''

He did overhear, Ceilidh thought, thoroughly embarrassed.

''Let us worry about that, Nev,'' Al said sarcastically and plunged his spoon into the milk and crisps.

"Of course, *Constable*. Far be it from me to keep you from your simple pleasures." Neville Brinkley turned on his heel and left the kitchen abruptly.

"Now look what you've done!" Ceilidh barked when the professor's slippered footsteps had faded upstairs. "You've insulted a man who could well be evaluating my work! Don't you realize a professional standing could be at risk here?"

"I definitely do," he said, meeting her angry eyes with a look that silenced her and brooked no comebacks. "But I'm not about to compromise the responsibilities of a friendship for it."

"I don't understand," she responded limply, the teeth having suddenly gone out of her anger.

"Maybe someday you will," he said. He took another spoonful of cereal and arose. "I have to go now."

He carried his cup and bowl to the sink and rinsed them before putting them into the dishwasher. "See you tonight," he called as he went out the door.

Jason was late for school that morning and Ceilidh was just about to call the teenager's home to check on him when he arrived, bedraggled and so pale she doubted the child had seen either rest or food since he had last left school.

As soon as class was under way, she left the other children engaged in a writing exercise and motioned the teenager to follow her into the kitchen. There she put two slices of bread into the toaster and took a quart of orange juice from the refrigerator.

"Sit down, Jason," she said softly, taking a jar of peanut butter from the cupboard and placing it on the table.

"I'm not hungry, Miss . . ." he began to protest but she hushed him.

"I never said you were. Just take care of this food while I go back to class, will you?"

She left the sullen-faced boy alone but when she peeked back into the kitchen a couple of minutes later she saw him ravenously bolting down toast and juice. It was then she decided to call Social Services.

Chapter Seven

Ceilidh finished marking the last exercise book, added it to the stack on the kitchen table, and stretched. It had been a long day, beginning with stable duty and ending now, at nearly nine o'clock with checking math problems, but an extremely satisfying one, she decided.

Neville's praise the previous evening had inspired her to take more initiative with her most difficult students. Toward that goal she had called Trevor's mother during the noon break and diplomatically explained her thoughts on the little boy's erratic behavior. To her surprise and delight, the child's mother had taken her advice and agreed to make an appointment with their family doctor to have her son examined for attention deficit disorder.

Then, encouraged by this indication of progress, Ceilidh had telephoned Karen Blackwell. She was completely elated when the director agreed to have Ben tested by an expert on learning disabilities.

Jason's improved behavior, however, had been the sweet topping on her day. She felt a smile tugging at her lips when she recalled how this change had come about and was no longer ambivalent concerning Constable Al's share in this metamorphosis. She was simply grateful. With the help of two remarkable men her career seemed to be falling into place.

For a few moments she sat savoring the high points of her day and enjoying the quiet of the country night. It was a cool evening, threatening frost, and she had lighted a fire in the potbellied stove. It gave off a homey, crackling warmth that Ceilidh found pleasant and comforting. She felt relaxed and happy.

In fact, she thought with a tinge of guilt, she was even glad Neville was not about to disturb her refreshing solitude. He had gone directly to bed after eating a light supper. He wasn't feeling well because of his cold, he had said, and furthermore the medication he had gotten from the doctor that afternoon was making him drowsy.

How sick can he be, she found herself wondering uncharitably. He's only got a cold. Then she chided herself on her lack of compassion. Some people have low tolerances to any illnesses, she reminded herself.

She was wondering if a cup of coffee at that hour would keep her awake, when car lights turned in the drive. Looking out the window she saw a vehicle she recognized as Al's Jeep bouncing up the rough driveway. He left his police cruiser at the RCMP office and commuted to and from the farm in his own vehicle. Ceilidh was glad. She didn't want to be forced to look at any more RCMP paraphernalia than necessary.

Shortly he was coming in the back door and Ceilidh had to squelch her initial reaction of gladness at seeing him. His appearance, however, instantly erased any selfish concerns she might have had.

"Al, what's wrong?" she asked, getting up quickly and going to him.

His handsome face was grim and haggard, exhaustion mirrored in every line.

"I'm okay," he said and went to the sink to get a glass of water.

"No, you're not," she said gently. "Tell me."

He sank wearily into the rocking chair, glass in hand, looked up at her, and tried to muster a grin.

"The fire feels good," he said. "Reminds me of evenings spent in the kitchen at my parents' farm."

"Al," She could feel his hidden distress and knelt at his knee. "Talk to me."

"There's been a car accident," he said. "A little girl was seriously injured. I worked to revive her but the ambulance was slow arriving."

"Al, she didn't . . . ?" Ceilidh's voice was shaking with emotion.

"No," he shook his head tiredly. "They say she'll be okay. But, Ceilidh, I was scared . . . really scared. And now I'm tired . . . so tired. Not much of a credit to the force, am I?"

"You certainly are!" She took his hand

and saw it was dirty and bloodstained. "You saved a life tonight. You'd do no less if you had it to do all over again right now. I'm proud of you, so very proud!"

"You're really good at this," he said softly and smiled wanly down at her. "Who taught you how to care for wounded Mounties?"

"No one." Ceilidh started as if he had pinched her and jumped to her feet. "I just . . . care about you. You're my friend."

"Well, well," he said, a semblance of the old teasing Al coming back into his tone as he looked up at her. "We are making progress."

"Now don't get carried away," she said, seeing he was recovering. "Have you had any supper?"

"No," he said.

"Well, go wash up and change and I'll make you a plate of cold chicken and potato salad. A couple of cups of strong coffee won't hurt you either. Now go, go."

She waved him away and headed for the refrigerator.

"Ceilidh?" She heard him get out of the rocking chair but kept herself occupied in the search for food.

''Yes?'' she asked from the depths of the refrigerator.

''Thanks.''

She turned just in time to see his broad-shouldered form going out of the kitchen toward the stairs. Pausing for a moment, she felt herself suddenly overwhelmed with compassion for the good, decent man Constable Allan Dumont truly was. Then another emotion fluttered up in her heart and instantly terrified her.

No! she cried inwardly and scrambled desperately to rip it out before it could take root. No, no, no!

She dove back into the refrigerator and rifled madly through its shelves as she tried to make her quest for chicken and potato salad the most important goal of her life.

She was setting the food on the table a few moments later when she heard another vehicle coming up the drive; a noisy vehicle whose driver seemed intent on gunning its engine to the hilt. Glancing out the window, she saw a dirty white pickup truck skid to a halt in the bright circle created by the back porch light. A bear of a man got out and lumbered angrily toward the door.

Well over six feet tall, barrel chested, his

features obscured behind a bushy red beard and long, scraggly hair, the stranger wore a faded jean jacket, plaid shirt, dirty khaki pants, and knee-high rubber boots. A blue bandanna was tied, biker fashion, around his head. Ceilidh jumped as his fist pounded on the door.

''Teacher? I'm Trace Reynolds, Jason's uncle. I want to talk to you!''

''Just a moment, Mr. Reynolds.'' Ceilidh felt slightly relieved to know the visitor's identity but realized she was not about to have an easy parent-teacher interview. As she steeled herself and opened the door, she was glad Al was home.

''Won't you come in, Mr. Reynolds?'' she said as pleasantly as she could muster and still keep the tremor out of her voice. ''I'm Ceilidh Highland, your nephew's teacher. I'm glad to meet you.'' She extended her hand but he refused it and pushed past her into the kitchen.

''Nice place you got here,'' he said coldly, scanning the room before turning small, bloodshot eyes on her. ''Jas and me got a good place to live too. Not as fancy as this but good enough. There was no need for you to call in them geeks from Social Services.''

''Please sit down.'' Ceilidh felt her knees growing soft but managed to force a smile and offer a chair. ''We need to talk about Jason. He's a good boy. He deserves a chance. . . .''

She didn't get an opportunity to finish. A big muddy booted foot shot out and kicked the proffered chair across the room.

''Talk! Seems you've already done more than your share of talkin' today!''

A hamlike hand swept out to grab Ceilidh by an arm. Al's voice stopped Trace Reynolds's move in midair.

''Something I can help you with, Trace?''

Framed in the parlor doorway, Al still wore the pants of his uniform but above the waist only RCMP-issue V-necked, long-sleeved underwear. He looked wonderfully tall and calm and powerful although his gun belt and holster were missing.

''Heard you moved in here, Mountie.'' Trace Reynolds faced Al squarely but it was apparent some of his bravado had fled. ''Must be real cozy.'' He glanced significantly at the police officer's state of undress.

"What can we do for you, Trace?" Al advanced into the room, cool as ice and just as hard.

"You can tell this interfering little witch to leave me and Jas alone!" he barked. "I won't stand for them joes from Social Services nosin' around my place!"

"Jason's a fine boy." Ceilidh, strengthened by Al's presence, determined to make the most of the moment for her student's benefit. "Won't you sit down and discuss his options with me?"

"Options? Yeah, right!" He turned and stomped toward the door. There he paused and swung back on the pair. His arm shot out and he pointed an accusing finger at Ceilidh.

"Stay out of my nephew's life, teacher lady, or you'll be sorry! I swear it!" Then he slammed out of the house.

"Trace, wait!" In five long strides, Al was across the room and out the door after him.

Through the kitchen window Ceilidh saw Al overtake Trace Reynolds beside the latter's pickup truck in the outer circles of the porch light. There, Al paused, clasped his hands behind his back, and in spite of Reynolds's flaying arms and face flushed red with fury, appeared completely unruffled and intent only on listening to the man's tirade. He seemed a perfect target for the big man's wrath.

Al, wake up! Ceilidh cried in her heart. *Be ready to defend yourself! Forget those police academy instructors who told you calm and nonthreatening is best! Quiet courage isn't the answer!*

Then, suddenly, her worst fears were realized. Trace Reynolds swept a huge hand inside the front of his jacket. He's got a knife . . . or a gun! Ceilidh's heart screamed. Al . . . Al!

Chapter Eight

When Trace Reynolds pulled a paper from his jacket and waved it wildly about under Al's nose, Ceilidh's entire body went limp with relief. Rolling her eyes upward, she gave heartfelt thanks.

Then, returning her attention to the drama unfolding in the dooryard, she saw Al take the paper, examine it for a few moments, and then return it to Reynolds with an affirmative nod. Trace snatched it up, stuffed it back into his jacket, and with a few words Ceilidh judged from his expression to be derogatory, climbed into his truck. A moment later he whirled the vehicle about over the lawn, tearing up grass and sod, and headed at a reckless speed down the driveway.

Al watched him go, then turned and walked back into the house. Ceilidh met him as he stepped inside, her face registering the kind of anger only absolute relief can trigger.

"You fool!" she half screamed. "You crazy fool! He might have had a gun . . . or a knife! Yet there you stood in the ridiculous 'at ease' stance, fairly asking to be injured or killed!"

"But I wasn't, was I?" he said with a calmness that irritated Ceilidh still further. "Trace only wanted to show me a paper that gave him temporary guardianship of Jason. Jason's parents were killed in a motorcycle accident last year and since the boy had no other living relatives Trace got custody, whether he genuinely wanted it or not. As for your fears, I've known Trace Reynolds for quite a while . . . he's never carried a weapon beyond those big fists of his. At least give me credit for being able to evaluate a situation and act appropriately."

"You're an idiot!" she cried. "A fearless, total idiot! I could . . . I could . . . !"

"Could what, Ceilidh Highland, what could you do?" He took her unexpectedly into his arm as she sputtered out her terror. "Kiss me?"

Brown eyes met brown eyes and something magic sparkled between them. Ceilidh found she couldn't protest when Al lowered his head and covered her lips with his a moment later.

"Al, I don't . . . want to . . . don't want to," she stammered, trying to come back to reality, to catch a steadying grasp on her suddenly slippery resolve.

"Don't want to get involved with a Mountie," he finished for her.

"Yes," she breathed. "I can't, I won't."

"But what about Allan Dumont, the man who cares about you?"

With an effort so intense she felt it sapped the last of her flagging strength, Ceilidh pulled free.

"*Constable* Allan Dumont!" she cried as she backed away from him toward the parlor door, small hands clenched at her sides. "The man and the Mountie are one and the same. And I won't get involved with him! Not now! Not ever!''

Then she turned and fled up to her room. There she flung herself on her bed and longed to sob out her tangled feelings. But she knew she couldn't. Neville was in the room across the hall and although probably soundly asleep under the influence of his cold medication (he hadn't been aroused by all the commotion below so she felt safe in assuming the associate professor was well out of the way) she didn't want to take chances.

Twenty minutes later she heard Al's booted footsteps coming up the stairs and was doubly glad she had managed to restrain herself. *He mustn't know, he must never know . . . I think . . . I know . . . I love him.* She let the terrible admission tumble into consciousness for the first time and was horrified.

Al's footsteps were slow and heavy, completely out of character from the brisk, authoritative stride he normally exhibited. Was he hurting too? she wondered. Were his attentions more than just the result of shared experiences and proximity?

She clinched her fists in her lap and

stared out into the tarpit of the moonless night beyond her window. No, she told herself. No.

His footsteps paused outside her door. Ceilidh's breath caught in her throat. Was he going to knock? What would she do if he did?

Her fears left as quickly as they had arrived. Al continued on to his room.

Lying in bed a half hour later, however, Ceilidh found herself in a quandary of emotions. Through the wall, in a closet of a room, the man she now had to admit she loved with every fiber of her being lay ensconced in a narrow, quilt-covered bed, virile, vulnerable, and completely wonderful. She pulled the blankets over her head and tried to quell her thoughts with another image.

On the polished top of the antique nightstand beside his bed, no doubt, lay his polished brown belt and the holster that housed his service revolver. It represented Al's career, a career she wanted no part of. Not now, not ever.

Hopelessly she pulled herself up on one elbow and vented her frustration by pounding her innocent pillow to a pulp.

* * *

The following morning Ceilidh lingered in her room as long as she dared. She hoped Al would leave before she had to encounter him but when constant glances out her window at his Jeep told her this was not to be the case, she finally realized she had no choice but to face him. Slowly she started for the stairs.

"Hi," she said cheerily as she stepped into the kitchen wearing tan dress pants, a green silk blouse, and her gold chain. She prayed she could keep up the charade of casualness until she grabbed something to eat and got out of the house.

"Good morning," he said, turning away from the percolator where he had been getting a cup of coffee. Apparently not on duty that morning, he was wearing jeans, a plaid shirt, and riding boots. He gave no indication that anything was wrong but the usual twinkle was missing from his brown eyes. "I hope you slept well."

"Yes," she lied and went to get a cup of coffee also as he sat down at the table with his cereal box and a bowl. "Did you?"

"Fitfully," he replied.

There the conversation ended. Feeling extremely uncomfortable, Ceilidh put her cup on the table and went to get a bowl and spoon.

"May I share your cereal?" she asked, sitting down opposite him and realizing she was catching his formality.

"Certainly." He was immediately the polite, courteous Mountie. He half arose and sprinkled cereal generously into her bowl. "Excuse me, please, for not offering. Milk?"

"Yes, please." Ceilidh said correctly. Then, because she could stand it no longer, blurted out, "Al, about last night . . ."

She didn't get time to finish. At that moment Neville joined them.

"Good morning, all," he said brightly. "You'll be pleased to hear my cold is completely gone. I'm feeling fit as the proverbial fiddle."

Ceilidh glanced quickly at Al. The professor had left himself wide open for one of the Mountie's sarcastic comebacks.

"I'm pleased to hear you're feeling better," Al astonished her by replying. "A cold can make a person very uncomfortable."

Al, Al, where are you? she almost cried. *This isn't you!*

Then the Mountie arose, carried his cup and bowl to the sink, rinsed them, and put them into the dishwasher.

"I'm going to town today," Neville continued, reaching for his box of what Al had called roots and twigs. "Do either of you need anything?"

"If it wouldn't inconvenience you too greatly, I'd like a liter of orange juice and a loaf of whole wheat bread," Al replied reaching for his wallet.

"No problem, Constable." Neville seemed pleased with Al's metamorphosis and was actually smiling at him.

"Thank you kindly." Al placed money on the cupboard by the door, put his wallet back into his pocket, and pulled a jean jacket over his plaid shirt.

"I'll see you this evening," he called back as he turned to leave. The next moment he had opened the door and disappeared into a deep autumn fog that was swirling about the dooryard.

Later as she drove to school in the heavy mist, Ceilidh was fuming. She didn't like the new Al but what had she expected? She had told him there was no hope for them romantically; he had simply respected her decision and walked away. Not even friendship would be possible now, she realized, hurting bitterly. He had asked for more and been refused. Today he had made it clear he would not accept any halfway measures.

Two tears slithered down her cheeks. *I want to love you, Al, I do, I do,* she thought. *But I won't, I can't!*

But her pain was just beginning, she was soon to discover.

"Are you going to the dance this Friday, miss?" Jason asked Ceilidh during the noon break the following day. "It's at the community center—a fund-raiser for Constable Al's swimming program. We need money for bus rental and gas and—"

"And pizza," Emma chimed in.

"Yes, and pizza," Jason went on. "Everyone's going."

"I . . . I don't know." Ceilidh was not herself that morning. She had slept little the previous night and, as a result, had gone to school feeling headachy and worn.

"It wouldn't look good if the teacher didn't support the program." Jason surprised her by keeping at the subject. Even though the teenager had improved greatly in his behavior toward her in the past week, this was the first time he had shown a desire to keep a conversation going.

''No, I suppose it wouldn't,'' she said slowly.

''You could get him to take you.'' Jason gestured at Neville Brinkley, who had just arrived at school and had come to join them.

Ceilidh was further amazed. From the first day Neville had come to school, it had been obvious Jason didn't like him. Now he was setting him up with a date.

''Get him to take Miss Highland where?'' Neville looked down on the child through mirrored sunglasses.

''This Friday night you could take Miss Highland to the dance to raise funds for Constable Al's swimming program,'' Jason embarrassed Ceilidh by explaining. ''It's at the community center with a country-western band . . . you don't even have to dress up. Everyone can wear jeans and T-shirts. You really should go . . . supporting students and all.''

Neville hesitated for a moment and

Ceilidh felt herself growing warm with humiliation. He didn't want to take her, she thought, and was trying to come up with an excuse.

"Friday night, you say?" he said finally and smiled. "Well, why not? It sounds like a pleasant enough diversion. What do you say, Miss Highland?"

Facing Jason's challenging blue eyes and Neville's unreadable ones behind the reflections in his lenses, Ceilidh could see no escape.

"Well, all right," she agreed.

Pleasant enough diversion, she scoffed inwardly, however. *How could I ever have fancied this stuffed turkey?*

"Great!" Jason was triumphant. "And just wait until you see who Constable Al is taking! She's a total babe!"

Chapter Nine

When Ceilidh arrived home after school on Friday, she saw Al's Jeep parked in its usual place. Neville's red sports car was missing, however, and she recalled the professor had said he was going grocery shopping. Probably he'd had to buy spinach, yogurt, and tofu, she thought sarcastically, then quickly gave herself a reprimand. Neville Brinkley had a right to be any kind of health food aficionado he chose. It wasn't his fault that he didn't share her food philosophy of good, old-fashioned nutrition liberally mixed with fun and enjoyment.

Fun and enjoyment. She looked at Al's Jeep and felt an analogy forming. No, she told herself as she went into the house and put her schoolbooks on the kitchen table. *I told him where I stand, he accepted it, so that's that.*

From upstairs a familiar male voice was vigorously blasting out snatches of the *Barber of Seville.* She shook her head helplessly and started for the stairs. He definitely didn't seem to be heartbroken over her rejection of his attentions. Good, she tried to tell herself. She had nothing further to worry about.

As she reached the top of the stairs she realized the lusty baritone was issuing from the open bathroom doorway and hoped Al was at least partially clothed or in the shower with the curtain discreetly drawn. He wasn't exactly shy about parading himself about in various states of undress.

He wasn't in the shower but he was dressed up to the waist in well-fitted, faded jeans Ceilidh discovered as she tried to pass the bathroom without glancing surreptitiously inside. He was barefoot, however, and wiping the remains of shaving cream from his smooth jaw. The room's humidity and several wet towels indicated he had recently showered.

"Hi." He stopped her, grinning. "You seem in a great hurry for a Friday night. Going riding?"

"Yes . . . no . . . maybe," she stammered as he turned to lean provocatively against the door frame, a towel draped over his broad, bare shoulders. "Are you?"

"No," he said. "I'm taking the kids to town for their water safety lesson. I decided to shower and shave first. I won't have time to do that when I get back. I'll have to pick up my date for the dance."

"Oh . . . yes, of course." Ceilidh felt slapped. "I hope you have a nice evening."

"I'm sure I will," he said, turning back into the bathroom and opening a bottle of aftershave. "She's a fantastic lady." He tapped out a few drops, rubbed the liquid over his hands, and proceeded to pat it liberally over his jawline.

"Well, try to avoid too much close dancing." Ceilidh was suddenly, uncontrollably furious. "Otherwise, you'll asphyxiate her with that stuff!"

She whirled and marched across the hall

to her room. Once inside, she swung back on him, her eyes snapping fire. "And please stop that caterwauling! You're not Pavarotti, you know!"

Then she slammed the door and flopped down on her bed hating Constable Allan Dumont and herself equally.

After she had calmed down, she decided she would go riding. She had to burn off some of the pent-up emotion that was threatening to consume her before she could even consider going to that dance. And listening to Al continuing to sing as he prepared for his date was more than she could bear.

It was lonely on the beach. A cold, northeast wind smashed white crested waves onto the pale sand with relentless abandon. Overhead a solitary white herring gull circled beneath billowing gray clouds. Once in a while, it would swoop low over the young woman on the horse and utter a strange, cackling cry that sounded like derisive laughter.

"Go away!" Ceilidh yelled finally, confident in her aloneness that no one would hear her inanity. "I know I behaved like a jealous fool! I don't need you to remind me!''

Then she turned Chance and galloped back toward the farmhouse.

Neville had returned, she discovered as she walked across the yard from the stable twenty minutes later. His car was parked in its usual place and when she hurried upstairs, eager for a hot shower after the cold, damp wind, she almost collided with him as, clad in a robe and slippers, he stepped out of the bathroom. The gust of mist that followed him told her he had just showered.

''Hi,'' she said.

''Hello.'' He smiled behind foggy glasses. ''What time would you like to leave for the dance?''

''Around eight?'' she said, wishing she hadn't made the commitment.

''Excellent,'' he said. ''I've already had a light supper. And I've showered. That leaves me a couple of hours to read over some research material before we have to leave.''

''Fine,'' she said and proceeded into her room. Read, read, research, research, she thought. Tonight would be about as much fun as a statistics seminar.

Oh well, it's for a good cause, she tried to tell herself as she paused before her mirror and looked at the wind-blown young woman in faded jeans and barn coat reflected there. Jason had said Al was taking a "total babe," she recalled, shoving her hair up on top of her head in a semblance of a new style. She grimaced at the result and let it fall back into place. *Well, I'll show Constable Allan Dumont Ceilidh Highland can be a total babe too!*

She undressed, wrapped herself in her thick, ankle-length terry robe, and padded into the still steamy bathroom. Step number one, a shampoo and shower.

She was working thick, creamy lather into her hair a few minutes later when suddenly the flow of hot water turned warm, then cool, then ice cold.

"Yiiiiiii!" she cried, fumbling frantically to turn off the taps. When she had succeeded, she grasped her soapy head in both hands in dismay. She knew what had happened. The ancient water heater had blown another fuse. Two long, hot showers had been too much for its advanced years.

And even once the fuse was replaced it would take two or three hours for the gasping old appliance to bring its temperature back to normal.

''Oh no!'' she breathed, already beginning to feel cold and sticky. She knew her shampoo would start to harden any second. All hopes of being a total babe for the dance vanished.

The moment Al stepped into the community center with his date on his arm, Ceilidh felt her heart sink. Sporting a California tan and exuding a vivaciousness that suggested a personality as attractive as the packaging, Jennifer, Al's companion, was willowy, blond, blue-eyed, and totally gorgeous.

Well, she tried to recover herself and be reasonable. What kind of a girl had she expected Allan Dumont to date? The young woman with the Mountie appeared to be the perfect complement to his exceptional good looks and swashbuckling personality. Forcing herself to turn away from the couple who were apparently lost in the hilarity of some shared joke, she smiled at Neville and tried to ignore the annoying soap itch that was threatening to overpower her resolve not to scratch any part of her poorly rinsed body.

She touched the ponytail at the back of her head and heard a crackle of static electricity. Without the benefit of conditioner, her hair was alive with the stuff. Realizing such gestures only incited more activity in her unruly coiffure, she quickly lowered her hand.

"Shall we find a place to sit?" she forced herself to ask her companion pleasantly and wished he wasn't wearing a tan designer sport shirt and coordinating light brown pants. He looked completely out of place in the jeans- and T-shirt–clad crowd filling the room.

"Excuse me?" Neville had been gazing over the crowd in the hall, green eyes intently focused on one person after another. "Oh, yes, certainly." He pulled his attention back to his date and smiled down at her. "Over here, not too near the band, if you don't mind. I'm not a great fan of country music."

"Okay," Ceilidh agreed but chafed at his admission. Hour by hour she was gaining more and more evidence that the man she had once considered someone special definitely wasn't . . . at least not in her books.

They had barely taken two chairs at a table for four near the back of the hall when a familiar voice made Ceilish whirl on her seat.

"Mind if we join you?" Al, one arm draped companionably about his date's shoulders, was grinning down at them.

Before Ceilidh could speak, Neville, like a true gentleman, was on his feet.

"Of course not," he said with alacrity and moved with amazing speed to pull out a chair for the beautiful blonde. "The more the merrier."

Ceilidh flinched inside. Couldn't an academic like Neville Brinkley come up with something more original?

"Good." Al saw Jennifer comfortably settled in the chair and turned to the group. "I'll get us something to drink."

"Soft drinks, Constable," Neville interjected quickly.

"Of course." Al bowed mockingly to the professor. He winked at Ceilidh and started for the bar. The old happy-go-lucky Al was back, it seemed, and the reason was his beautiful date.

Ceilidh watched his tall, broad-shouldered form wending its way carefully through the crowd and felt such a deep sense of loss that her stomach heaved. He would never be hers. But, then, hadn't she made that decision? With an effort so great she felt its pain in her heart, she returned her attention to the man and woman sharing the table with her.

"Well, Miss . . . ah . . ." Neville was saying and glancing significantly at Ceilidh.

"Wishert, Jennifer Wishert." The young woman smiled. "Ceilidh can't introduce me since she and I have never met. Allan seems to have left us to introduce ourselves."

"Neville Brinkley," the professor quickly made himself known. "And this, you apparently already know, is Ceilidh Highland, the teacher at the local school."

"I'm glad to meet you," Jennifer said, flashing perfect white teeth in a wide, welcoming smile. "Please call me Jen. My friends all do."

Charm, charm, charm, Ceilidh thought. *Darn! But what do I care? She can have Constable Allan Dumont and his high-risk lifestyle!* She looked back at Neville Brinkley and tried to smile. He returned it absently, apparently again absorbed in registering people and faces in his mind.

"Is anything wrong?" she asked.

"No, no." He pulled his attention back to her. "Sorry if I seem a bit distracted this evening. I've got my mind on my thesis and can't seem to let go."

"Would you prefer to go back to the house?" Ceilidh was exasperated by his reply. This was turning out to be a really wonderful evening, she thought sarcastically.

"Definitely not!" He roused himself. "I'm going to forget work right now and enjoy myself. Miss Wishert . . . Jen, what do you do?"

"I'm the secretary at the local RCMP station," she replied. "And you, Neville?"

"I'm an associate professor currently on a sabbatical to write a thesis on one-room schools and their sociological and educational advantages and disadvantages."

"Impressive." Jennifer Wishert looked genuinely interested. "You've certainly taken on an ambitious project. It must have immense historical value since most of our grandparents were products of the one-room school system.''

''Definitely.'' Neville Brinkley's eyes lit up behind his glasses. ''You've grasped my concept entirely.'' He leaned forward over the table in Jennifer Wishert's direction. ''Allow me to explain further.''

Great! Ceilidh leaned back in her chair and let their animated conversation flow past her. Miss Charm and Beauty would have both men before the night was over. Why hadn't she, Ceilidh, had the good sense to stay home?

Al returned with their drinks and sat down opposite Ceilidh. She felt his gaze on her and tried to avoid his eyes but then he spoke to her and she was forced to look over at him.

''New hairdo, Miss Highland?'' he asked, reminding her of the unwanted ponytail bouncing at the back of her head. His eyes were twinkling mischievously. Ceilidh felt like yelling at him.

''No.'' She tried to be nonchalant but touched her hair self-consciously. Her gesture set up a crackling and sent errant strands bristling out from her head.

''Oh,'' he replied in apparent innocence.

"I was afraid our water heater might have let you down, pesky thing that it is."

"Of course not! I had a wonderful shower." She was appalled to hear herself lying.

Then, just as quickly, she felt an overpowering urge to scratch her back. Ignore it, she ordered herself. Just ignore it.

The moment Al turned his attention to Jennifer, however, Ceilidh could no longer bear the annoyance. She fidgeted as discreetly as possible in her chair, easing her discomfort against the rungs of its back.

"Anything wrong?" Al had instantly turned back to her. "You seem in some sort of distress. Is there anything I can do?"

"No, I'm fine, just fine." Ceilidh sat bolt upright and fought to will herself not to itch. "These chairs take a bit of getting used to, that's all."

"Really?" He was dead serious. "I find them quite comfortable."

She wanted to kill him.

A few minutes later, still miserably uncomfortable and wishing more fervently than ever that she had stayed home, she watched Al and Jennifer gyrating around the floor in time to a wild, fun-filled country song. The couple was having so much fun, she found watching them as irritating as the dried soap on her body. *How ridiculous,* she chided herself, and turned back to her date.

"Let's dance," she invited Neville and started to rise. She'd show that exhibitionist who called himself a Mountie a thing or two about sensuous dancing.

"I'm sorry," Neville refused apologetically. "I'm not very good at this kind of thing. The next waltz, perhaps."

"Fine." Disappointed Ceilidh sank back onto her chair. Then, feeling eyes on her, she looked across the floor and filled with chagrin. Al Dumont was looking directly at her and must have seen Neville's refusal of her invitation. How humiliating.

"Excuse me, I'm going to the ladies' room," she said abruptly and hardly allowed Neville time to lift himself politely off his chair before she darted away.

By the time she had made her way through the crowd to the washroom, the music had stopped. As she reached to push open the door, she nearly collided with

Jennifer Wishert, who was headed in the same direction.

"Oops! Sorry," the blond woman said and laughed. "Going my way?"

She held the door open for Ceilidh to precede her. Once inside she pulled a slender comb from her jeans pocket and ran it needlessly through her wonderfully carefree-looking hair.

"Whew!" She grinned at Ceilidh, who was making an effort to be similarly involved in grooming. "It's warm out there! Hard to believe it's a frosty night outside. Winter is really on its way, I guess."

"Yes." Ceilidh had to struggle not to like the pleasantly friendly, unaffected young woman. She's genuinely nice, she thought bitterly.

"Would you like to go to town shopping some Saturday?" Jennifer startled her by asking. "Since you're new to the area, I could show you around."

"That would be nice," Ceilidh, unable to think of an excuse, heard herself replying.

"Great! I'll call you." Jennifer stuck her comb back in her pocket, wrinkled her nose derisively at her reflection in the mirror, and waved good-bye. A moment later she had disappeared back out into the milling crowd.

Feeling totally exasperated with the way the evening was going, Ceilidh followed. She stepped back into the dimly lit hall just as the band struck up one of her favorite tunes.

I'd love to dance, she thought unhappily. *But there's no point in asking that stuffed shirt I came with.*

The next instant her wish came true. A strong brown hand seized her and swung her out onto the floor. Astonished, she suddenly found herself face-to-face with Allan Dumont in the middle of a room full of rollicking dancers.

Within seconds she was having a great time. The sensuously deep, rushing rhythm of the tune wrapped around her and she let herself be swept away. Ceilidh was a graceful, natural dancer and when she glanced over at Al, she saw appreciation of the fact mirrored in his expression.

''Go, Cail!'' he said and laughed as he moved smoothly in response. Ceilidh forgot her resolve and laughed too. This was the Al she knew and loved. And how she had missed him! To be back with him was as close to heaven as she would ever come on this earth, she knew.

When the song ended, she returned to earth with a mental thud. Swinging away from Al's mischievous, fun-filled eyes, she tried to make a fast retreat back to the safety of their table. Al, however, had other plans and was quicker.

The band had shifted easily into a waltz and just as easily, he caught Ceilidh by the hand and swung her into position in his arms, against his hard body.

"I've got to get back to Neville," she tried to protest, shocked as before by the sensations physical contact with him sent racing through her.

"He's fine." Al leaned close to her ear in order to be heard above the crowd and music. "Look."

Ceilidh looked. And saw Neville Brinkley apparently deeply involved in conversation with Jennifer.

"Yes, I guess he is," she said, sighing, and allowed Al to whirl her across the floor until she found they were alone in a darkened corner of the hall.

"Al, no!" she protested as his arms fell

about her until they were locked behind her slim waist. Helplessly she looked up at him, unable to continue. His hands began to massage her back gently, easing away that horrendous itching. Involuntarily she sighed.

"Feel good?" he asked softly.

"Oh, yes!" she breathed, unable to control the intense feeling of relief his actions had inspired. She relaxed in his arms and sighed again.

"Ceilidh," he said, his voice husky with emotion. "Oh, Ceilidh."

She looked up into his brown eyes and was lost. Slowly, carefully he drew her against him until their bodies moved together as one in time to the romantic rhythm of the song, until his lips were against her ear.

Intoxicated by the moment, Ceilidh slid her arms up and around his neck. The hot, smoky room seemed to vanish and they were alone in their wonderful world of majestically whirling emotions and intense feelings.

"I've missed you," she whispered, his nearness making her senses reel, the unyielding wall of his powerful body melting her resolve to wait for someone special, someone safe, like a snowball in a microwave.

For a few brief moments Ceilidh floated in the dreamlike existence that was Allan Dumont's embrace. Then, abruptly, the music stopped. Simultaneously Neville Brinkley's voice destroyed the illusion.

''I believe Miss Highland is *my* date, Constable.'' The professor's voice made her fairly leap from Al's embrace.

''Now, just a minute . . .'' Al tried to pull Ceilidh back to his side but she pushed him away, resolve and common sense returning. Neville *had* brought Jennifer to the dance, hadn't he? And only two nights after he had been romancing her in the farmhouse kitchen.

''He's right, Al,'' she said, although her knees had turned to jelly and she heard her voice as high and squeaky as that of a trapped mouse. ''The dance is over anyway. You should be getting back to *your* date. Let's go, Neville.''

Turning on her heel, Ceilidh marched with as much strength and dignity as she could muster away from what she knew would always be one of the best days of her life.

Chapter Ten

The drive back to the farmhouse was, for Ceilidh at least, accomplished in an uncomfortable silence. Neville appeared lost in some kind of intense thought. Was he considering the suggestive position in which he had discovered her and Al? Was he deeply upset? Or was he simply, once again, contemplating his thesis?

Then she realized she didn't really care anymore. Neville Brinkley had lost all his appeal in her eyes.

At the house he bid her a polite but cool good-night and went immediately to his room. Weary hearted, Ceilidh followed him upstairs slowly and decided the water would be hot enough for a decent shower. Heaven knew she desperately needed one to quell the terrible physical discomfort she had endured all evening.

Hot water and steam didn't help her inward irritation, however. Standing under the spray of water, vigorously shampooing her hair, she was haunted by visions of the laughing brown eyes and broad shoulders of the most enjoyable, exciting man she had ever known. Abruptly she finished rinsing her hair, turned off the water, and stepped out onto the bath mat.

As cool air touched warm skin, she shivered and thought how much it felt like pulling out of Al's embrace less than an hour ago. Trying to rid herself of such troubling comparisons, she toweled her hair and body vigorously and pulled on her thick terry robe and slippers.

On her way back to her room she noticed there was no shaft of light under Neville's door and assumed he had gone directly to bed. Soft, barely audible strains of a Mozart concerto, however, wafted from behind the closed panel. *Probably trying to cleanse his system of the effects of all that country music,* Ceilidh thought sarcastically and then shook her head woefully as she entered her own room and shut the door. A few days ago she would have been applauding Neville Brinkley's choice of music, his cool reserve. Now, suddenly, everything about him seemed wrong and annoying and everything about Allan Dumont seemed right and completely wonderful. Love does make one crazy she thought.

Going to stand before her dresser mirror she removed the towel from about her head and slowly began to brush out her tangled hair. Then, pausing, she leaned closer to her reflection. *I'm not beautiful like Jennifer Wishert,* she thought. *My nose is too short and my cheekbones aren't nearly high enough . . . And as for my mouth . . .*

Abruptly she stopped. It was pointless. It didn't matter who was the fairest in the land. She, Ceilidh Highland, was not about to compete with any woman for Allan Dumont. She was an independent woman with a challenging career, a career she had planned and worked toward for many years. She wasn't about to let a man, a

Mountie, transform her into an emotional wreck.

With that resolved she snapped off her light and went to the window to look out at the full harvest moon hanging like a giant, glowing beach ball over the barn. Below the fields and trees were dark and mysterious, haunted by shadows as deep and incomprehensible as Ceilidh's feeling. She found the scene soothing, however, in its quiet peacefulness and curled up in the window to savor it.

Al would be home soon. He had left the dance with Jennifer the same time she and Neville had headed back to the farm and, since the young woman lived only a few houses from the community center, it wouldn't take him long to deposit her at her door. She'd just wait. After all, she couldn't go to bed until her hair was dry, could she? She pulled her slippered feet up onto the seat and hugged her knees.

Ceilidh awoke with a start. It was beginning to get bright outside. Dawn, she realized, surprised. She felt stiff and cold and cramped. She must have fallen asleep and spent the night huddled in the window seat.

Getting to her feet, she stretched and

fluffed her now thoroughly dry hair. Then, yawning widely, she made her way to the door. *Coffee, I need a nice hot cup of coffee,* she thought dully.

She was halfway downstairs when she came fully awake and recalled her reason for waiting in the window seat. She paused a moment, then shrugged and continued to the kitchen. Why had she decided to do such a foolish thing, she wondered as she reached for the coffeepot. Allan Dumont was a big boy. He didn't need anyone to wait up for him. Morning had a way of putting a whole new complexion on things. Romantic notions generally fled with daylight and birdsong.

With the coffee on to perk, she walked to the window and gazed out at the vehicles parked in the yard; Neville's red sports car, her own modest Sundance, and . . . and that was it, she realized with a shock. Al's muddy gray Jeep was missing! And there were no fresh tracks in the frost laying white over the drive to indicate he had returned and left again.

There was only explanation. Al hadn't come home all night.

For a few moments she could only stare

at the empty space where Al normally parked. Then a weak, sick sensation flood over her. Al hadn't been on call last night so duty hadn't taken him away. Jennifer Wishert's beautiful face flashed across her mind and a muted little cry of sheer agony escaped her lips.

All thought of coffee fled. She had to get away from the excruciating pain suddenly ripping into her heart.

She rushed back upstairs, flung on her riding clothes and a slicker, and raced out to the stable. There she saddled a sleepy, startled chestnut mare, led her out into the first hard, cold drops of a wind-whipped autumn rain, and vaulted onto her back. Lunging the horse seemed pointless. No riding mishap she could imagine could wound her any more severely than had Al's failure to come home.

As she allowed Chance to break into a restrained lope and headed for the beach, she was thankful for the rain slicing down over her face. It disguised her tears.

As horse and rider burst out onto the shore, Chance was prancing, throwing up her head and snorting. Guiltily Ceilidh realized the little mare was sensing her mistress's agitation and tried to relax.

"Sorry, girl," she said, patting the mare's drenched neck. "It's not your fault. Take it easy. We're going to be"—she hiccupped—"just fine."

Chance slowly relaxed into an easier trot. Ceilidh knew, however, that her mount was still anxious, keyed to her rider's unsettled emotional state.

Twenty minutes later Ceilidh was holding Chance to a trot along the beach, when above the crash of waves and howl of wind, she heard a shout. Turning in the saddle, she saw Al on Special racing after her.

"Okay, you've been wanting to run, now run!" Ceilidh told the eager little mare and put her heels to her sides.

Chance was off in a bound, stretching swiftly into a full run along the rainswept, stormy beach. Bent low over the mare's neck, intent on her riding, Ceilidh dared glance back only once. Through her hair, splashed wet and dripping over her face, she saw the Mountie and his horse rapidly gaining on them.

"Run, Chance, run!" she yelled.

The little mare stretched again but she

was no match for the gelding's longer, more powerful strides. Al and Special were bearing down on them, the sound of pounding hooves told Ceilidh but she wasn't about to give up.

Al's next move, however, caught her totally by surprise. Suddenly, as he came abreast of her, he swept out a powerful arm, caught her around the waist, and pulled her from her mount into his saddle in front of him.

Before she could regain herself, she was dropped unceremoniously on her feet. Beside her, Al reined to a sand-raising halt and leaped to the ground. He was drenched, his dark hair tangled and hanging raggedly over his forehead. Although it was bitterly cold he was dressed only in the T-shirt and jeans he had worn to the dance. More evidence that he had been out all night. That he must be nearly frozen also flashed across her mind, then vanished into her pain and outrage.

"You, you . . . !" she found herself sputtering inanely. "You idiot! What do you think you're doing?" And was glad it was still bucketing rain. He couldn't see her tears.

"I've seen it done in old movies for years." He grinned a little sheepishly. "It looked really romantic . . . and, Ceilidh, I'm really trying to be romantic right now."

"I just bet you are!" she cried. "Were you also being romantic with Jennifer last night . . . when you didn't come home? And . . . what happened to your face?" Her anger faltered as she became aware of a large purple bruise over his left eye and deep scratches down his cheek beneath.

"Nothing much . . . all in the line of duty," he said, brushing her inquiry aside. "Now, listen to me, please!" He caught her by both shoulders and shook her gently. "We have to talk, really talk, Ceilidh Highland!"

"Why? Because you're an overbearing, interfering . . ."

"Probably I have been but it's only because I love you."

A bolt from the blue could not have silenced Ceilidh any more effectively or completely.

"You . . . what?" she finally managed to squeak.

"I love you, admire you, respect you,

need you!'' He was looking deep into her eyes, his expression tense with emotion. ''Do you understand?''

''But Jennifer . . . ?'' She was still too dazed to take it all in.

''Jennifer's engaged to the crown prosecutor in town,'' he said. ''George, her fiancé, couldn't make it to the dance yesterday so Jen agreed to go with me in an attempt to make you jealous. I'd planned to go right home afterwards, sweep you into my arms while you were still smoldering with rage, and explain how I felt. Only—''

''Only you decided to stay with Jennifer!'' Ceilidh, her fury returning, tried to shrug free but found herself pinned in his iron grip.

''No! Listen, will you? I ended up being part of a sting operation which included a drug bust at Jason's uncle's place. That's where I got this face. Trace Reynolds hit me with a piece of chain.''

''At Jason's home?'' Ceilidh was horrified. ''What happened to Jason? Is he all right?''

''He's fine, probably better than he's been in a long time.'' Al quieted her wide-

eyed fears. ''He's asleep in my almost finished apartment. Susan made him take a
hot shower, fed him a hearty meal, and then
tucked him in as lovingly as if he were her
own child. Nate says she and Harry will
have no trouble getting custody, which is
what they plan to do.''

''Nate who?'' Ceilidh was growing more
confused by the minute.

''Nate Birchmount, better known to you
as Neville Brinkley,'' Al astonished her by
explaining. ''He's an undercover RCMP
officer, drug squad. I recognized him that
first day in your drive and did a double
take. He's probably the best officer in his
field . . . a consummate actor who can be
anything from a college professor to a
tramp . . . but he's completely remorseless
in any relationship he needs to establish to
accomplish his purposes. He's left broken-
hearted women behind him wherever he
goes. Ceilidh, he used you, your walks on
the beach, the dinner overlooking the bay
as surveillance opportunities. Remember
how he wanted you to wear a dress when
you went for a walk that night he found us
barrel racing? He wanted people to be con-

vinced it was romance he was after, not drug smugglers.''

''No!'' she cried, trying to wrench free. ''You're making this up! It's all too incredible!''

''Sweetheart, listen, please!'' Al held her unrelentingly and finally she ceased to struggle against his superior strength. ''That window over your front porch was ideal for his purposes. All those nights you thought he was soundly asleep, he'd let himself out over the porch roof and wasn't there at all. Instead, he was prowling the beaches in search of evidence. And when he finally had it, he decided to draw the net . . . last night after the dance. That's why he insisted on soft drinks, remember? We had to be at our best later. We must have been because we managed to capture a fair number of drug dealers and smugglers.''

Ceilidh felt herself going limp in Al's grasp. *This is crazy,* she thought, her mind reeling. *Neville is an undercover agent, Jason's uncle is involved in drug trafficking . . . and Constable Allan Dumont loves me. No, no, no, I can't accept all this! I won't!*

''I don't believe you!'' she cried. ''This is too incredible. . . .'' But she did.

Her words were shut off as Al caught her to him and covered her lips with his. The sensation, so sudden and startling, found Ceilidh completely off guard. Reflexively she responded with her heart and soul. Her arms flew up and about his neck and in the cold rain and wind with the crashing waves as their background music, they held each other passionately, enraptured by the magic of their love.

"Ceilidh," he muttered finally against her wind swept hair. "I love you so, Ceilidh."

She longed to reply in equal terms of endearment but the words froze in her throat as memory and reason crashed in over sensation and emotion. Nothing had changed. He was still *Constable* Allan Dumont, RCMP.

"Let me go, Al," she forced herself to say evenly. "I don't want this . . . I don't want to be involved with you." She touched his injured face gently with trembling fingers. "And this is the reason."

"What?" Astounded, he held her away from him so that he could look down into her face. "Ceilidh, what are you saying?"

"I loved an RCMP officer once." She

choked hoarsely, dropping her arms and backing away from him. ''He almost died from a gunshot wound suffered in the line of duty. I vowed I never would suffer like that again. And I won't.''

She turned and headed back to where Chance was standing, ground tied and dripping, farther down the beach. She wondered if she would have the strength to climb back onto her mare and ride away, her heart was aching so severely, her emotions racing so intensely.

With a soul-wrenching effort she gathered up Chance's reins, stumbled into the saddle, and cantered past Al and Special homeward down the beach.

''Ceilidh, wait!'' he yelled as she rode past. ''I think I sprained my back when I lifted you off your mare! I'll need help getting into my saddle.''

''That will teach you to pull ladies from their horses like a macho fool!'' she flung back at him and galloped away.

As she turned Chance up the shore's incline toward the trail that led into the trees, she glanced back and saw him far back in the distance leading Special up the beach. He was limping.

I'm being cruel, the cruelest I've been in my life, leaving him alone and hurting, she thought. *But it's the kindest thing I can do for him right now. I can't offer him a commitment and he should be free to find someone who can, with no regrets or empty hopes from the past to inhibit him.*

Nate Birchmount was waiting for her in the farmhouse kitchen. Dressed in full RCMP uniform, he seemed an entirely different person from the university professor he had been impersonating. Neville Brinkley was gone, probably forever; he had, in fact, never existed. This tall, blond, good-looking police officer was reality.

"I'm sorry I had to deceive you, Ceilidh," he said as she pulled off her slicker and began to stuff paper and kindling into the potbellied stove.

She was shivering uncontrollably both from the cold and from her shattered emotional state. She desperately needed the warmth and cheerfulness of a wood fire.

"Here, let me do that," he said gently, taking a card of matches from her shaking fingers. "I made coffee while I was waiting for you to return. You look as if you could use a cup."

Ceilidh turned the fire making over to him and arose. As he knelt before the stove's front opening, she went to the percolator and poured herself a steaming cup of rich, dark liquid.

"Please sit down." Nate Birchmount said, rising once he had a blaze crackling in the stove. "Let me explain."

"Constable Dumont already has," she said, sinking down into the rocking chair near the fire's warmth. She wrapped icy fingers around the coffee mug and took a shaky sip.

"Then you know it was all in a good cause," he said, looking down at her. "Ceilidh, I never meant to hurt you, please believe me. But I needed you."

"As a cover," she said, looking unblinkingly up at him.

"Yes. And for what it's worth, I'm sorry." He went to the door, then turned back to the young woman huddled in the rocking chair. "I packed while you were out. I'm leaving for a new posting. I wish you much success in your career. From what I've observed and from my actually sketchy knowledge of educational matters,

I'd say you're well on your way to becoming an excellent teacher. I hope we meet again someday, Ceilidh Highland. It's been a distinct pleasure.''

He paused a moment, seeming to deliberate, then continued slowly. ''Try not to judge Constable Dumont too harshly for his part in this matter. He's an excellent officer who managed to behave professionally throughout the entire operation in spite of his feelings for you. You'd be amazed to know how many times he reprimanded me when we were alone for my attentions toward you and warned me to behave decently. Since I'm his superior in rank, he was risking disciplinary action each time he spoke out. I thought you should know.''

''Are you going to report him?'' Ceilidh was instantly deeply concerned. After the emotional pain she had just inflicted on him, she couldn't bear to think she had hurt him professionally as well.

''No.'' He shook his head and smiled faintly. ''It's not considered insubordination for an officer to fall in love.''

Then he left. Ceilidh watched his red sports car go down the drive and pull out onto the highway. Then, clutching her coffee cup, she dashed upstairs to her room. She couldn't bear to see Al when he returned.

Chapter Eleven

Ceilidh dialed her parents' telephone number and waited impatiently as it rang and rang. It was 7:00 A.M. Sunday morning. She had not seen Al since they had parted on the beach the previous morning.

When he had arrived back at the house she had stayed in her room, listened while he showered and changed, then heard him leave. He had not returned. Later, when she discovered his clothing and other personal belongings were gone, she had assumed he had gone back to stay at RCMP headquarters and would contact her later to explain. But he hadn't. Now, confused and hurting

163

after a sleepless night, Ceilidh desperately need her parents' support and advice.

"Mom?" Ceilidh's voice sounded high and childish when her mother finally answered.

"Ceilidh, hi! It's good to hear your voice, dear," came the quick, cheerful reply. Then, "Is anything wrong? You sound different. And, good heavens, it's only 7:00 A.M.!

"I'm fine," she replied without much conviction in her tone. "How are you and Dad?"

"Wonderful, thanks. We just got back from a trip around Nova Scotia's Cabot Trail. Ceilidh, you really have to go sometime. The scenery is magnificent! Your father took roll after roll of film and I steeped myself so deeply in the ambience, painting from his pictures will bring back memories of pure delight this winter. Now, what's new with you? There's something going on, I can tell. There always is when you telephone instead of e-mail."

"Mom, were you ever sorry you married Dad?" Ceilidh blurted out the question more suddenly than she had intended.

"Sorry? No, of course not! Whatever made you ask such a question?"

"But didn't his job worry you? Weren't you ever afraid of losing him? Mom, tell me the truth. Remember I saw you on nights when he was late back from work. I saw . . ." Her voice was rising treacherously high.

"Ceilidh, Ceilidh, of course I worried." Her mother's voice was soothing. "But the alternative is unthinkable."

"Alternative?" Ceilidh felt she was losing the trend of the conversation.

"Never having had him to worry about," her mother said softly. "Now, come on, child, where is all this leading?"

"I've met someone." The confession seeped out of Ceilidh like repressed steam. "And, Mom, he's an RCMP constable!"

"Ceilidh, that's wonderful! Your father will be so pleased! When can we meet him?"

"But, Mom, I'm so confused. There was this other man . . . an academic I thought I wanted . . . safe, settled . . . only he turned out to be neither an academic nor right for me. Then along comes Constable Allan Dumont, devil-may-care and all, and I think . . . I know I love him. How could I fail to recognize anyone that special?''

''You didn't. You only failed to admit it. And, honey, forgive me for saying this, but you wouldn't make a suitable wife or even companion for any mundane man. You're Ceilidh Highland, clever and caring but also as fun loving as your name suggests and as high-spirited as a thoroughbred. You'd drive a quiet, retiring man to distraction.''

''Mom!''

''It's true, my darling. Anyone who has seen you ride or dance knows that. Now get off your high horse and go capture that man before it's too late.''

''Take it easy, Mom. There's nothing definite, no commitment. I'm . . . I'm just . . . investigating the possibilities.''

''Now you sound like your father,'' her mother said with an amused chuckle. Then she became serious. ''Honey, just answer me one question: Do you love him, really love him? Can you imagine life without him?''

''Yes, no, maybe . . . oh, Mom, I'm so confused.'' Ceilidh was exasperated. ''I thought I had my life all figured out; a nice safe life with no unnecessary risks, no un-necessary worries. I thought I knew exactly the kind of man I could love and form a relationship with. Then he came along . . . not at all what I'd imagined and yet . . .''

''And yet you've fallen in love with him.'' Her mother's voice was aglow with pleasure. ''I'm so happy for you, sweet-heart. Love is life's greatest reward.''

''But, Mom, he's RCMP!'' Ceilidh's voice rose again. ''He'll be dealing with criminals and accidents and danger for the rest of his life! I could lose him in a heartbeat!''

''We all are vulnerable to losing people we love in an instant,'' her mother said gently. ''Some of us perhaps more so than others, it's true. But we can't allow fear to keep us from celebrating life. And certainly it's meant to be celebrated . . . with some-one special if we're very, very fortunate.''

''But the risks—''

''Honey, do you remember when you fa-ther first wanted to teach you to ride? Do you remember how reluctant I was to allow it?''

''Yes,'' Ceilidh said slowly, wondering

where her mother was headed with this train of thought.

"And do you remember how I acquiesced the first time I saw you trotting proudly around the paddock on that pony. You were so happy I knew it was worth any risks involved. And I was right. Would you have been happier never learning to ride, never knowing what your father calls 'the joy of a full canter'?"

"No," she said with conviction. "No, I definitely wouldn't have been."

"Well, then . . ."

"Mom, you do know what you're advising?" Ceilidh asked cautiously. "He is a constable in the RCMP and plans to make the force his lifetime career."

"I most certainly do, my darling." Her mother's reply brooked no room for argument. "Ceilidh, be proud of him. He belongs to a long tradition of heroes. Be proud such an honorable man has chosen you." Then her tone lightened. "I assume he has expressed himself?"

"Well, yes, sort of. That is, he tried to . . . I think . . . but I haven't given him a chance."

"Ceilidh Highland! Don't tell me you've

been putting him off simply because of his work! I'm ashamed of you. And I can't think what your father would say!''

''Yes, I was.''

''Well, then, my darling, hang up the phone this instant and go to him! Your father and I will be waiting to hear your news. Good-bye.''

The line clicked and went back to its normal, monotonous buzz. Slowly Ceilidh replaced the receiver and stood up. Her mother and her heart had given her answer. She grabbed a jacket and ran outside, determined to find Al and tell him she'd been a cowardly fool, that she loved him madly, wildly, to distraction. Then she remembered the horses.

They hadn't been tended yet that morning. She couldn't leave them unfed. It would only take a minute; she headed for the stable.

When she entered the barn, Ceilidh was surprised to hear a familiar voice talking to Special. The door of the gelding's box stall was slightly ajar and, looking inside, she saw Jason busy with a manure fork, talking soothingly to the horse as he worked.

''Hi, Jason,'' she said. ''What are you doing here?''

''Tending the horses,'' the teenager said, pausing and leaning on the fork. ''Corporal Aimes dropped me off at the end of the driveway awhile ago. He told Constable Al he'd drive me over twice a day to look after Chance and Special while he's gone.''

''Gone?'' Ceilidh was astounded. ''Al is gone? Where? To town?''

''No, gone to work somewheres else,'' the boy said and snapped his bubble gum. Startled, Special snorted and stamped his front hoof. ''Easy, boy,'' Jason said, patting the horse's sleek side, and Ceilidh, even in her state of shock, was impressed with how far this once belligerent child had come under Al's guidance.

''Where exactly is somewhere else?'' Ceilidh tried to keep the urgency out of her voice.

''Dunno.'' Jason returned to cleaning the stall. ''Halifax, maybe. Anyway, he left with that Neville Brinkley guy around ten o'clock last night. I helped him pack his Jeep.''

''But he must have said when he was

coming back.'' She pressed more fervently than she wanted to.

''Nope.'' Jason lugged a forkful of manure past her out of the stall and deposited it in a wheelbarrow. ''They're sending a new guy to take his place tomorrow.'' He stopped, then and looked at Ceilidh, his freckled face concerned and serious. ''But it won't be the same, will it, miss? That Constable Al, he was someone special.''

Chapter Twelve

It had all the makings of a green Christmas. Ceilidh stood by her classroom window and looked out at the bay, cold, black, and grim in the overcast day. Along its edges, shards of ice hung in ragged disarray as they waited to extend their frozen dominion across its entire expanse. Bitter gray clouds hung low to meet the icy water along the horizon. On the shore, marsh grass lay bent, stiff, and brown from last night's subzero chill. Ceilidh sighed. Her heart felt as cold and forlorn as the world outside that window.

Al had been gone for two months and

not once during that time had he called or written. Ceilidh had taken to checking her e-mail twice daily on the school computer in hopes he would contact her through that medium but there was nothing, only her daily messages from her mother and father.

Then, one cold, rainy evening two days ago, desperately lonely, she had e-mailed her father and asked him as casually as she could if he would use his connections with the RCMP to locate a Mountie formerly posted to the Bay River area. He had been especially close to the children and they would like to send him a Christmas card, she had explained. Although she wasn't actually lying to her father (her students had made Al a huge Christmas card) she knew it wasn't her main reason for seeking help in finding the constable and felt a tinge of guilt at deceiving her dad.

Her father had replied that he would try. As yet, he apparently had had no success.

''Miss?'' Jason brought her out of her reflections as he joined her and held up a tinsel star. ''Is this okay for the top? Trevor wants it there and if you say it's okay, I'll get the step ladder and put it up to satisfy him.''

Ceilidh brought herself back to the present and smiled at the eager teenager. The children were trimming the school Christmas tree and Jason was particularly eager although he tried to mask his enjoyment by using the younger students' enthusiasm as an excuse for his willing participation in the task. Ceilidh wondered if this was the first Christmas tree Jason had ever trimmed and felt her heart ache for all the child must have suffered before his beloved Constable Al had come into his life.

"I think that's a good idea," she said. "Let the little ones trim the bottom and the windowsills. Emma and Johnnie can work on the branches above them, and you and Ashley can trim near the top." She knew Jason secretly had a crush on twelve-year-old Ashley and would welcome the chance to "be made" to work alongside her.

"Great!" Jason started to leave eagerly, then paused and turned back to his teacher.

"Miss?" he asked a bit awkwardly.

"Yes, Jason?" she replied, absently fingering the blind cord.

"Could you smile a little more often? Constable Al said you were prettiest then . . . and he was right."

"I'll try." She forced her lips up at the corners. "There, how's that?"

"Great." He grinned. "Keep the thought."

Then he returned happily to the tree trimming. Ceilidh felt her smile spreading naturally as she watched him go.

With his uncle in jail, the teenager had a new life. He lived with Harry and Susan Aimes and for the first time was discovering what it was to be a member of a caring family. He had even become deeply devoted to the couple's infant daughter, Elizabeth.

Adding to these advantages was the fact that he also had a part-time job caring for and exercizing Special and Chance, who were still stabled at the farm. Every two weeks Jason received money to cover his wages and pay for the needs of both animals. When Ceilidh questioned the teenager as to the source of this income, he had merely shrugged and said Corporal Harry gave it to him, sent by Constable Al through RCMP courier service from an undisclosed location.

Ceilidh had shuddered at this information. Had Al gone into the doubly dangerous world of undercover work, perhaps with the deceptive Nate Birchmount? Would he someday turn up on a list of unknown bodies?''

She couldn't bear to think about it and vowed to forget Constable Allan Dumont for the one millionth time since he had left. She had her students, her amazing little students. Surely that was enough for any teacher. All thirteen of them had been making steady progress, each in his or her own unique way over the past months, and Ceilidh was proud.

Karen Blackwell had visited a week ago and had had nothing but praise for her young protégée and her work.

''The parents are extremely happy with their children's results,'' she had said, smiling and standing at the front of the classroom. ''And the students certainly look content. The Department of Education cannot help but see the merits of small, rural schools after this. I feel thoroughly vindicated, and I have you to thank for it, Miss Highland.''

Ceilidh had been delighted. Praise from an admired superior was wonderful stuff.

An hour later, when the children had finished trimming the tree and were working in their scribblers, Ceilidh looked up from checking a math exercise book at her desk and caught Jason whispering conspiratorially with Ashley and Emma.

"Jason, this is work time," she reproved gently. It was no longer necessary to be forceful with her nicely behaved students. "If you finish soon, we'll have time to read the rest of our Christmas story before lunch."

"Yes, miss," he replied but cast Emma a long, slow wink before he turned to bury himself in his writing scribbler.

Emma's little face was bright with some sort of inner joy and she suppressed a giggle as she too returned to work. Ceilidh felt her suspicions rising. What were they plotting?

Music from the *Nutcracker Suite* was drifting softly from the stereo a half hour later as Ceilidh finished reading Dickens's *A Christmas Carol*. The children clustered on the floor about her as she sat in one of the window seats in the library. They had listened so attentively she was glowing with a feeling of success.

"That was a pretty good yarn, miss," Jason said, clearing his throat.

Ceilidh smiled at him and knew he could identify with a child's hardships.

"I think so too," she replied.

"Pretty good?!" Emma was indignant. "It is beautiful . . . it's a classic!"

Ceilidh smiled even wider at the little girl's description. *I have gotten through to them,* she thought.

Then she glanced at her watch and realized it was nearly lunchtime, time for her to slip into the kitchen for a moment and turn on the burner under the pot of soup the Department of Education provided each day to accompany the children's brown bag lunches.

"You can browse through some other books for the next few minutes," she told her students. "I'll start lunch."

She had just arisen when she glanced out the window and saw a heart-stoppingly familiar gray Jeep pulling into the school parking area. It halted and a familiar tall, broad-shouldered, and handsome RCMP officer wearing a winter-issue fur hat, navy overcoat, and high polished boots alighted.

Astounded, Ceilidh stood frozen among her students.

A moment later the front door opened and Constable Allan Dumont stepped inside. He swept his hat from his head, smiled at Ceilidh, and instantly the dull December morning was dazzlingly bright and vibrant.

"Hello," he said simply. Then he turned to the children. "Hi, kids."

"Hi, Constable Al!" they cried in delighted unison.

"Hello," Ceilidh managed a bit more slowly.

Then the room went silent. Not a child stirred. Finally Jason, unable to contain himself, spoke.

"Well, go on, Constable. Do it."

Al touched his forehead in a salute to Jason and, as the children parted to make way, proceeded across the room to where Ceilidh stood. There he dropped on one knee before her.

"Miss Highland, will you marry me?" he asked.

Ceilidh felt the room spin. She looked down into Al's dazzling smile and wonderful brown eyes and for a moment believed she was dreaming.

"Miss Highland, I'm asking you to marry me, here before witnesses," he repeated and took her hand in his.

"Say, yes, miss, oh please, say yes!" Emma grasped Ceilidh by the other hand. "It's soooo romantic! Think of the story I can write about it!"

"He's a good man, miss." Jason spoke in the most manly tones his changing voice could muster. "You'll be hard pressed to find better."

Still dazed, Ceilidh looked around at the expectantly eager faces of her students, then back down at Al. With brown eyes at once twinkling with mischief and wickedness, then slowly dissolving into deep caring and painfully cautious hope, the man kneeling before her reached out and forever captured Ceilidh Highland's heart. He was definitely someone special. She drew a deep breath.

"Yes," she said.

A cheer went up from the children. As Al rose and drew Ceilidh into his arms, Emma pointed to the window and clapped her hands in delight.

"Oh, look!" she cried. "It's snowing! And Miss Highland has her someone special. It's going to be a perfect Christmas!"

"But . . . I don't understand," Ceilidh stammered. "Al, what are you doing here?"

"I came on the advice of your parents," he astonished her by replying with a heart-tipping smile. "When you sent me packing that day, I wasn't about to give up. I just needed some time to regroup and investigate this mysterious Mountie you said you loved and who had discouraged you from ever loving one again. Through the force, I learned you were none other than the daughter of John Highland, one of the most respected officers the RCMP has ever had. I was incredibly stupid not to have made the connection myself.

"I then got in touch with your parents. Great folks, by the way . . . it'll be a pleasure being their son-in-law."

"Please get on with it!" Ceilidh was growing exasperated with excitement.

"Well, your mother told me about your call . . . that did wonders to strengthen my resolve to marry you, by the way . . . but both she and your father advised me to wait, to let you stew in your own gravy, as your dad put it, until you had time to cool off and realize how you felt about me, how much you missed me.

"I took a temporary job exchange with a friend of Nate Birchmount's in Halifax. Your father said he'd let me know when I should come back. Your e-mail two days ago told him the time was right. He immediately sent one off to me. 'Now' was all it read.

"I came back late last night and stayed at Harry and Susan's. That's how Jason knew I had returned and became a coconspirator in my plans. I told him what I intended to do but warned him to secrecy." He turned to the proud teenager. "Thanks, pal. I knew I could trust you."

"No problem, Constable." Again Jason employed his deepest tone. "Come on, kids. It's time for lunch. Miss and the constable want to be alone."

The teenager took command and began to herd the children toward the kitchen. When the rest of the students had left the library, he paused in the doorway and looked back at the couple by the window.

"I was wrong, Miss," he said, grinning.

''You do know someone special when you see him.''

Then he left the room whistling softly. This time Ceilidh didn't try to stop him.